Westward Wagons

Westward Wagons

Cheri LePage

ReadersMagnet, LLC

Westward Wagons
Copyright © 2023 by Cheri LePage

Published in the United States of America
ISBN   Paperback: 979-8-89091-255-8
ISBN   eBook: 979-8-89091-256-5

All rights reserved. No part of this publication may be reproduced, stored in a retrieval system or transmitted in any way by any means, electronic, mechanical, photocopy, recording or otherwise without the prior permission of the author except as provided by USA copyright law.

The opinions expressed by the author are not necessarily those of ReadersMagnet, LLC.

ReadersMagnet, LLC
10620 Treena Street, Suite 230 | San Diego, California, 92131 USA
1.619. 354. 2643 | www.readersmagnet.com

Book design copyright © 2023 by ReadersMagnet, LLC. All rights reserved.

Cover design by Tifanny Curaza
Interior design by Dorothy Lee

TABLE OF CONTENTS

CHAPTER ONE **7**
May 1892 .... *7*
CHAPTER TWO **19**
CHAPTER THREE **29**
CHAPTER FOUR **45**
Samantha & Cassidy *45*
CHAPTER FIVE **55**
Gwen & Tucker *55*
CHAPTER SIX **68**
Jillian & Skyler *68*
CHAPTER SEVEN **84**
Samantha & Cassidy *84*
CHAPTER EIGHT **89**
Andrea and Blake *89*
CHAPTER NINE **104**
Gwen and Tucker *104*
CHAPTER TEN **118**
Samantha & Cassidy *118*
CHAPTER ELEVEN **130**
Jillian & Skyler *130*
CHAPTER TWELVE **146**
CHAPTER THIRTEEN **164**
Andrea & Blake *164*

CHAPTER FOURTEEN **169**
Jillian & Skyler 169
CHAPTER FIFTEEN **181**
Andrea and Blake 181
CHAPTER SIXTEEN **191**
Jillian & Skyler 191
CHAPTER SEVENTEEN **195**
Andrea and Blake 195
CHAPTER EIGHTEEN **207**
Gwen and Tucker 207
CHAPTER NINETEEN **215**
Samantha & Cassidy 215
CHAPTER TWENTY **227**
EPILOGUE **233**

CHAPTER ONE

May 1892

The five covered wagons slowly rolled through St. Louis, continuing until they were just west of the city, stopping at a location that many other wagons had rested before. All of the occupants were tired from the many days of long hours of continuously traveling. The group would stay here for the rest of the day, taking a much-needed break from their journey on the Oregon Trail, but first thing in the morning, they would start on the next round of their intense trek.

The first wagon belonged to Jethro Delaney, the trail master. He found out over the years that stopping early one day every hundred miles or so, helped prevent the occupants from becoming too tired, which seemed to keep tempers from erupting. They usually stopped near a town so the travelers could buy needed supplies, wash their clothes, and time just to recuperate before starting out on another hundred miles of the trail.

This was his tenth year of trekking across this old trail and he wished it were his last. He was tired of these long lonely trips, weary of having to deal with all the different families, with their many unique personalities, and their never-ending complaints. He was fed up with trying to keep everyone in line, afraid he'd go mad if he had to put up with any more females like the four, he had on this trip, as these were the worse, he'd ever met in his life. If he survived this trip, he might give it all up and just stay in Oregon.

What made the situation terrible is sometime today four more wagons would be joining them, and the way his luck was running, the new women would be worse than the ones he already had. Why couldn't a woman be more like a man? Of course, a couple of the men on this trip had been creating trouble as well, but still they weren't as bad as the women were.

The second wagon contained Abe Combs, and his two spoiled and spiteful nineteen-year-old fraternal twin daughters, Faith and Florence Combs, who were always causing some sort of problem for the other women on the train. They were going to Oregon, where their father hoped to find them a husband before they drove him crazy.

Jethro thought the man needed a lot a prayers and money in order to find grooms for these two, as he doubted any man would be dumb enough to hitch themselves to either of these two witches. Of course, the right amount of currency in one's pocket could change a person's mind into marrying anyone, including someone like Faith and Florence Combs.

At the beginning of the trip, Abe had practically thrown his daughters at him, but Jethro told him that he was married to his job and didn't need a wife. Besides, he was old enough to be their father. Some men didn't mind marrying a woman that much younger than themselves, but he wasn't one of them, as he didn't need to raise a child. Jethro was relieved when Abe backed off, as he had his hands full with trying to keep everything running smoothly, and didn't need these two women chasing after him during their trip across the country.

Earl Vorbeck and his wife Ruth were in the third wagon, newlyweds who were also going to Oregon, with the hope to start a new life together. Jethro couldn't figure out why they'd married as they were both unquestionably unhappy in the marriage, but then it really wasn't any of his business.

They were a mismatched couple, as Ruth was an attractive woman, but Earl was what you would call butt ugly. Jethro didn't understand why Ruth or any woman would want to be married to such an unattractive man. Maybe if he shaved and took a bath, he would be more appealing to look at. Ruth was a jealous woman who made Earl's life unpleasant with her continuous nagging and complaining during the trip. She had a habit of running to Jethro every time one of the other young women on the wagon train happened to look at her husband. Earl was just as much as a problem as he flirted with anything in skirts, which Jethro was sure he did just to antagonize his wife.

The fourth wagon held Gerard Stolte, his wife Esther and their two young children, Calvin was ten, and Daisy was two years younger. Jethro thought they were the best well-behaved children he'd ever seen in all the years of having do this trip. The children were excited about going to their new home, as their father had promised them their own horses once they arrive at their destination, which was a cattle ranch in Fayette Missouri.

When they reached Boonville, the next rest stop of their trip, Gerard and his family would be leaving the train to travel to their new home, which was about thirty miles north of Boonville. Jethro would miss them when they left as he enjoyed watching the children play in the evenings with their father or helping with the chores.

The fifth wagon carried Brock Colligan and his two young daughters, Charissa and Jillian, two half-sisters, who were as different as night and day. They were going to Kansas City so Jillian could marry a rich man, one old enough to be her grandfather. Brock had sold her and Jethro was sure the money would be spent buying things for Charissa, which everyone in the wagon train knew was Brock's favorite daughter.

Jethro felt sorry for Jillian, who was a quiet and well-mannered young woman. Whenever Jethro saw her around her family, she appeared sad and lonely. Usually in the evening after she had done all her work, including work Jethro thought the older sister should be doing, Jillian would spend the rest of each evening with the Stolte family. Not once during this trip had he heard her complain about her workload, but Charissa on the other hand, complained if she had a hair out of place.

Jillian Colligan hated the thought of marrying a man she hadn't ever met before, especially one who was older than her father was and in poor health. All she knew about the man was he was an old friend of her father, and that in itself was enough to scare her.

With her experience of teaching at a one-room schoolhouse for a year, she was ready to leave her father's home, but before she could, her father decided to marry her off to some man as old as the hills.

As long as she could remember, her father had always favored her older sister and over the years, she'd learned to accept it. When her mother had been alive, Angela had been there to give her all the love and comfort she needed. But when Angela died suddenly, Jillian found herself alone for the first time in her young life. She was hurting from the loss of her mother, but Brock didn't care, as he was too busy catering to Charissa's every whim to worry about Jillian missing her mother.

Charissa was a spoiled and spiteful woman; one who had their father wrapped around her little finger and she made sure Jillian was aware of that fact. She was the reason why Jillian had to marry some old man, as she wanted Jillian somewhere where her beaus couldn't be distracted by her half-sister's beauty.

Charissa had wanted her sister to travel to Kansas City by herself, but Brock was afraid Jillian would run away instead of meeting her groom as planned. Therefore, since Brock wasn't going to leave Charissa at home while he took Jillian and her belongings to Kansas City, it meant she had to endure the trip as well. Charissa made sure Jillian knew it was all her fault she was on this awful trip instead of home with her many beaus, and did whatever she could to make Jillian pay.

Jillian learned early on their trip to stay as far away as possible from Earl Vorbeck. The first night out while she had been collecting firewood, he'd grabbed her so roughly, she was afraid he was going to attack her sexually. In order to get him to let go of her, she had to knee him in the groin, and ever since then, she made sure she wasn't ever alone with him. She didn't understand why he was interested in her, as she thought his wife was a more attractive woman than she was.

Whenever Ruth Vorbeck saw Earl near Jillian, she would run and complain to Brock that his daughter was after her husband. Jillian had to laugh at that one, as she thought he was so ugly that he made her skin crawl. Brock always assured Ruth that Jillian was spoken for and wasn't available for any man. Then once he returned to the wagon, he would beat Jillian to teach her to stay from the man.

Jillian also learned to stay away from the two Combs sisters, as they made her life miserable with their nasty comments and their dirty tricks whenever she went near them. She spent most of her free time, which wasn't much, visiting with the Stolte family, as they made her feel as if she was part of their family. She was actually thinking that when they reached Boonville, she would run away and go live with them after they left the train.

Just as the sun was setting that same day, four new wagons pulled into the area to join the first five wagons. As the new wagons drove into the field where they were to camp, the people from the first group watched with interest.

Faith and Florence were looking for any young single men joining them for their trek across the country, each hoping to find a husband among the new travelers. If not a husband, maybe a couple of tumbles in the man's bedroll, as both were experienced in that department.

Earl and Ruth Vorbeck also watched the newcomers' arrival, but each for a different reason. Earl was looking for a woman to fool around with since he couldn't get anywhere with Jillian, while Ruth was looking for adversaries for her husband's attention.

Jillian Colligan watched hoping for a man who would marry her and save her from the husband her father had planned for her, while her sister was looking for a husband for a completely different reason.

In the first wagon was Boone Farrell, a man in his fifties and his young wife, Andrea. Age wise, the pair looked more like father and daughter than husband and wife, and they were going to Oregon to start a new life there. Boone was a large man, with broad shoulders, and a belly so large, it hung over his belt. He had a cold stern expression on his face, one that just by looking at him a person knew to stay away from his very pregnant wife who sat next to him.

Those who watched them pass, saw a woman that looked like a frighten rabbit as her eyes stared down at her lap instead of observing the scenery around her. Her enlarged belly told a story of its own, as those who knew anything about childbirth, knew the baby would arrive before they got to their final destination.

Andrea's nightmare had begun the day her father forced her to marry Boone, and now that she was expecting a baby, it didn't look as if it was ever going to end. After the wedding, she'd refused to speak to her father as her husband had started beating her just minutes after their wedding vows had been spoken.

Her father had died recently, but she didn't mourn him, as she hadn't forgiven him for forcing her to marry this horrible man. She wasn't all that sure Boone hadn't had a hand in her father's death, as shortly after his funeral, Boone had packed up the wagon and they started westward.

The money she'd received upon her father's death, went directly into Boone's hands. She knew where he kept it, and if she ever got brave enough to run with it, it was enough for her to start a new life somewhere far from him. But so far, she been too afraid he'd come after her and beat her to death to give it a try.

With the end of Andrea's pregnancy being so close and having Boone as a husband, Gwen and Samantha, two of the women of their group, helped Andrea as much as they could. Andrea was touched, as their help make her life just a bit more bearable, and she was going to miss her friends when they went their separate ways.

She was glad she was too pregnant for her husband to make love to her anymore, as she hated his touch. Each night as he lay next to her, she prayed he would drop dead so she would be free of him, but so far, it hadn't happened. The thought of having Boone's child depressed her, because now she was tied to the man even more.

She wasn't afraid of being alone as she had some money hidden away, money she received from her father on her wedding day. It had been meant for her and Boone, but she had put it in her trunk and hidden it instead of giving it to her husband. At first, Andrea had been afraid Boone would get into the trunk and find it. But then, she quit worrying, for if he knew about the concealed money, he would have already confiscated it.

In the second wagon were Felix Atwood and his wife, Gwen, a couple from Tennessee, whose first child was due in four months. And just like the Stoltes, they were traveling with the wagon train just until Boonville, and then they too were heading to Fayette. Once there, Gwen would claim her inheritance from her maternal grandfather, Harlan Simpson.

Harlan had died recently leaving Gwen his home, which consisted of one hundred acres of rich grazing land, all the animals he owned, including the mare that had been Gwen's as a child. She couldn't wait to arrive, as his ranch had once been her home. She was sad she hadn't gotten the chance to see her grandfather one last time before his death, but after her mother died, she hadn't known where to find him.

She had lived in Fayette for most of her early years, as she and her mother; Margaret Rodgers had moved in with her grandfather after her father's death. Gwen had been too young when Norman Rodgers died to have remembered anything about her father, but each night as her mother tucked her into bed, Margaret would tell Gwen of their courtship and wedding. Norman had been a wonderful husband and father, and Margaret hoped someday Gwen would find someone to marry just as wonderful as her father.

When Gwen was twelve, her mother met Sherman Snyder and they fell in love, and decided to marry. When Margaret told her father she was going to marry Sherman, the two had a big fight. Harlan said if she married a man who was just after her money, he wouldn't have anything more to do with her and would even disown her.

Margaret married Sherman anyway and they moved away, of course taking Gwen with them. They had a wonderful marriage and she wasn't ever sorry for leaving with the man she loved. She didn't ever forgive her father for his harsh words the last time they spoke, nor did she ever correspond with him.

Two years ago, Sherman became sick and died, leaving Gwen and her mother without an income. Gwen tried to get her mother to write to her grandfather for his help, but she refused, saying she was sure the man was dead. Then less than a year later, Margaret passed away from unknown causes, leaving Gwen to believe her mother had died of a broken heart. Tears formed on her cheeks as she thought of how much she still missed her mother and stepfather.

When Margaret died, Gwen had to sell everything they owned *just* in order to bury her mother. She was didn't have any money and didn't have a place to go, so when Felix, a nearby neighbor, offered her marriage, she accepted. She hadn't wanted to marry him, but she didn't want to live on the streets nor did she want to work at the local whorehouse.

It wasn't until after she'd married Felix that she'd found out about her inheritance, but then it was too late to back out of the wedding. As soon as Felix heard about the inheritance, he quit his job and started making plans for them to move to Fayette.

She wasn't sure how her grandfather's lawyer had found her after all these years, but he had. She just wished she could have been the one to have to talk to the man who had been looking for her the past year, instead of Felix. For if she had, she would have taken the first stagecoach out of town, leaving her husband behind without even packing her bags or saying goodbye to him.

Drew, Corey, and Samantha Tyson, three siblings from Tennessee, made up the third and fourth wagon. They had lost their parents recently and were going to California to start their lives over.

Drew, the eldest, was the more serious of the two brothers, as it was now his responsibly to watch over his two younger siblings. Corey came next, who was more layback than his brother was, and Samantha at eighteen, was the baby of the family. She was small framed, which gave her the appearance she was a lot younger than she actually was.

There had been a great deal of love between her parents, and Samantha had promised her mother she wouldn't marry anyone unless the man could make her feel special and loved. Someone whose kisses made her body sing, and her spirit soar, just as her daddy had done for her mother.

Samantha had received several marriage proposals while they were still in Tennessee, but knew they weren't the right man for her, as when they asked her to marry them, she had a strong desire to escape instead of setting a wedding date.

When her older brothers decided to sell their childhood home to move to California, she was glad she had a valid reason to refuse each marriage offer she'd received. So, she pleasantly thanked them for their proposal, telling them she was sorry she couldn't marry them as she was moving to California with her brothers. None of the men was happy with her decision, but they accepted her refusal like the gentlemen they were.

CHAPTER TWO

The two Combs sisters frowned when they saw the gorgeous young single woman in the third wagon as it passed them. Jealousy filled them as they took in Samantha's beauty, but their frowns quickly turned to grins when they saw the two men coming up behind her, one was riding a horse, and the other was driving the last wagon in the group.

Charissa also smiled when she saw the two young single men joining the wagon train, as either one of them were perfect for what she needed. All she had to do was get one of them to take her to bed, then when her father found out about it, he would force the young man to marry her. Charissa just wanted a man to marry her, and any man would do as long as he was young, good-looking, and especially good in bed.

Ruth watched the wagons too, frowning when she saw the three young women joining their group, as she thought each of them were more attractive than she was. She knew just because two of the women were married and with child; it wouldn't stop her husband from looking or more, if the opportunity arose.

As the new group of wagons stopped and began settling for the night, the Combs sisters watched the two young men unhook the attractive woman's oxen before taking care of their own wagon. The two girls put their heads together to conspire how to cause mischief against the lovely young woman, not realizing she was the two men's sister, and not a rival for their attention. As the two sisters whispered together, they came up with a plot to take the young woman out of the running for the interest of the two young men, giggling at their brilliant idea.

Once the three Tysons were finished with their wagon, they went out to meet the other travelers. As they visited with the Stolte family, Drew and Corey quickly learned from Esther, that unless they were interested in getting married, to stay away from the two Combs sisters and Charissa Colligan. Since Drew and Corey weren't interested in marriage just yet, they returned to their wagon before meeting the three women Esther had mentioned, but Samantha stayed to visit when Jillian joined them.

Jethro went to each of the four new wagons to welcome the travelers. When he saw the two pregnant women, he wasn't happy, especially knowing Andrea Farrell would be delivering her child before the end of their trip. Traveling was hard enough on a woman without being in that condition, as too many things could happen on the trail. During almost every trip he'd been on, at least one person had been hurt in one accident or another and over the years, he'd seen more than his share of death along the trail.

He told Boone if his wife went into labor while they were traveling, she had better cross her legs because they weren't stopping until the end day. Boone didn't appreciate Jethro's words, but what could he say to the man since he was in charge and could prevent them from joining the wagon train if he so desired. Boone acknowledged his comment, then went to inform his wife about what the wagon master had told him.

When Boone informed Andrea that she couldn't go into labor during the day while they were traveling, she decided her husband was even dumber than she originally thought. Anyone who knew anything about childbirth, knew you couldn't plan when the baby came, or once labor started stop it on command or regulate how long it would take the baby to arrive.

That night was an extremely warm one, not even a breath of air moved. Corey was already under their other wagon, and being so warm in the wagon, Samantha decided to sleep outside with Drew, hoping it would be cooler.

Samantha brushed her long auburn hair, which she thought was her one and only good feature. Her hair was like her mother's, long, thick and exquisite. She hadn't ever thought herself as pretty, especially when she thought of how beautiful her mother had been. Remembering her mother brought tears to her eyes, but she quickly wiped them away as she needed to look towards the future with her brothers, not at the past and the death of their parents.

After Drew checked on the animals, he bedded down next to Samantha for the night. He told her good night and she responded back, then she closed her eyes and listened to the usual night sounds of fellow travelers readying for the night. Soon she was fast asleep.

It was late, and the sky was dark as the moon hid behind a cloud. As the coyotes howled in the distance, Faith and Florence crept to where Samantha laid under the wagon. Drew had left his pallet to go to take care of a call of nature, so when the two women arrived to do their dirty work, he wasn't there. In the darkness, they didn't notice the empty pallet of blankets beside her, so they still weren't aware of Samantha's relationship with the two men.

Faith took her scissors and very carefully began cutting off Samantha's beautiful hair. Florence snuck into the wagon to confiscate Samantha's dresses, frustrated in the darkness that she couldn't find any of them, she swore. She was just about to leave, but then the moon came out from behind the cloud, lighting the canvas enough for her to find Samantha's only two dresses. Florence hastily grabbed the items, hurriedly rolled them into a ball, and put them under her arm, then she crawled out of the wagon to join her sister.

The two sisters joined hands as they promptly ran off with smiles on their faces. Keeping close to the trees for the darkness they offered from the moonlight, they sprinted to the river and threw the dresses into the swift moving river.

They giggled at the thought of how the girl would react in the morning when she found both her hair and dresses gone. Not wanting to be found missing, they swiftly scampered back to their wagon, without anyone aware of their antics. Their father had slept the whole time so he was unaware they'd been gone or the mischief they had caused.

The next morning it was just starting to get light when Drew called out to wake his sister to start the day. Not realizing her hair had been cut off, Samantha started to move out from beneath the wagon. Just as she did, she saw the hair lying around her and threw her hands to the back of her head. When she touched it and found most of it gone, she screamed out an ear-piercing cry.

"Someone has cut off all my hair," she sobbed, holding the hacked strains in her hands as tears ran down her cheeks.

"Oh my!" Drew took one look at her chopped off hair and his heart broke. Instead of her lovely waist length locks, she had a chopped off shaggy mess on her head.

Corey ran to the wagon when he heard Samantha's scream, stopping quickly in his tracks when he saw what had happened to his sister's hair. I'm sorry, sis," he said, grabbing her for a hug. How could anyone be this cruel to another person?

"It isn't your fault," she said tearfully as she rested her head on his shoulder.

"Who would do something this horrible to you?" asked Drew as he tried to comfort his sister.

Gerard Stolte had joined them when he'd heard her scream. "I bet it was those two Combs's troublemakers. They most likely saw your sister, and thinking she was more beautiful than they were, they decide to do something mean to her," he responded to Drew's comment.

"If those two women think we would be interested in them after what they've done to our sister, then they're in for a big disappointment. Even if we weren't family, I don't want to become involved with any woman who would do something this horrible to another human being. This was more than just a joke, this was a vicious act," he said to the others around him.

"I'm lucky to have two wonderful brothers like you," she said through her tears.

"What is all the screaming about?" Jethro Delaney demanded as he joined them beside the wagon.

"Someone on this train cut off all of my sister's hair," Drew angrily told him.

"Why do you think someone on the train did it?" he asked, then frowned when he realized how stupid his question sounded even to himself.

Drew looked the man straight into his eyes. "Do you think some wild animal crawled by with a pair of scissors and did this?"

Jethro felt uneasy as the man stared at him. "I guess I could question the other travelers."

Gerard snorted. "I bet it was those two Combs girls," he told the wagon master. "I'm sure they won't be admitting to it."

"Unless you have proof, you best keep your opinion to yourself or you just might find yourself off this train."

Gerard laughed. "You don't scare me one bit. I paid my share the same as the other families have. You threaten to have me thrown off for stating the obvious, when Faith and Florence have been nothing but trouble since we started out on this trip. Just so you know ahead of time, I plan to report you to your superiors for the way you have handle the female problems on this trip."

"I've tried to keep things running smoothly. It isn't my fault we're having troubles with a few of the women."

"Well, you won't be having any troubles with the women who joined the wagon train last night. Mrs. Farrell, Mrs. Atwood, and my sister are very pleasant women," Corey told the wagon master.

"Good. Now get your breakfast started so we can get this day going. We're on a time table and I don't want to get a late start because of this hair problem."

"Aren't you going to do anything about my sister's hair?" Corey asked him.

"It's just hair. It'll grow back in a few months."

When Corey gave him a stern look, he cleared his throat. "I'll ask, but I don't expect anyone will take the blame."

It wasn't until Samantha went to get dressed that she found out her only two dresses were missing as well. Luckily, she had brought a pair of jeans and several blouses to wear or else she would have been traveling in her nightgown until they reached the next town, as they would leaving here before Boonville shops opened for the day.

Jethro stopped by Abe Combs' wagon to talk to him about his daughters, but Abe defended them, saying they didn't have anything to do with what happened to the young woman. After Jethro was gone, Abe threatened both his daughters to stay away from Samantha. If either of the girls did anything to get them kick off the train, they would both pay for it, and they didn't doubt for a moment he meant every word of what he said.

Sure enough, not one person claimed to know anything about the incident regarding Samantha's hair. Because of Jethro's investigation into her situation, the wagon train started out of St. Louis twenty minutes late that day, something that didn't sit well with Jethro. Trouble had already started with the other wagons joining them, and they hadn't even left St. Louis yet.

At first, Faith and Florence Combs were tickled at what they had done to Samantha, but when both men refused to have anything to do with them; they realized the two good-looking men were the young woman's brothers. They regretted their actions, as it had caused them to lose any chance, they may have had with the two handsome men.

Even though Corey and Drew weren't talking to either of them, it didn't stop the girls from scheming of ways to incise the men into their bed.

That night after they had finished their evening meal, Esther came over to try to repair some of the damage to Samantha's hair, but since it'd been cut so short, she didn't have much luck making it presentable. After Esther was done with her repairs, Samantha looked more like a young boy than the young woman she was.

Esther told Samantha that even with her hair so short; she was still the most beautiful girl on the train. Samantha blushed as she hadn't ever had anyone but family tells her she was beautiful. She didn't let the comment go to her head, as she knew how awful she looked with her hair hacked off.

Sam kept her hat on during the day, and didn't take it off until she turned in at night. Too afraid of sleeping outside, even though Drew assured her he would keep her safe from harm, she entered the wagon and removed the hat. After her nightgown was on, she brushed what little hair she had left, then laid down in the hot wagon, letting the tears come.

That same night, Charissa went for a walk, strolling slowly towards the Tysons' wagon, making plans for seduction as she went. When she passed the two young men, she pretended to stub her toe and fall, and they both quickly ran to her side to help her stand. She was ecstatic when they came to her aid, but was quickly disappointed, for when she told them her name, they quickly said good night and returned to their wagon.

She looked over at the Stolte wagon, betting her last dollar Esther had been telling tales to the new occupants of the wagon train about her. She felt like going over there and telling that woman a thing or two, but she quickly changed her mind. She didn't want to act up and have Esther run to the two men and tell them about the confrontation. She smiled, already planning what she would wear tomorrow to attract the men's attention.

The next day Charissa didn't have any more luck trying to get either one of the Tyson brothers alone than she had the day before. The situation was almost funny to watch, as whenever she walked towards one of them, it wasn't long after she reached him, that the other brother or even the sister would appear.

Charissa would give up for today, but she wouldn't get discouraged as she had plenty of chances before they reached Kansas City, as those Tysons couldn't always be together. The first time she found one of them alone, she would pounce on the opportunity to get one of them in a situation they would be forced by Pa to marry her.

The wagons continued to travel across Missouri, stopping only for the noon meal and two short breaks each day. As the days passed, the frustration of the different personalities of the women on the wagon train began to wear thin on all the men. Ruth, Florence, and Faith had taken an instant dislike to Andrea, Gwen, Jillian, and Samantha because of their beauty and they made sure everyone knew it. Charissa didn't think any of them were as beautiful as she was, so she didn't care one way or the other about the other women.

Esther Stolte was the only woman who became friends with the four attractive young women, and as she got to know them, she found even though they were beautiful, none of them had an easy life.

CHAPTER THREE

Cassidy Eldridge came upon wagon train as it traveled directly into the late afternoon sun. Wondering if this could be his uncle wagon train; he kicked his horse to the front of the train to find out. But when he saw the trail master, he realized this wasn't his uncle's wagon train as he'd hoped.

"Hello," he called to the man in the front wagon.

Jethro startled, as he looked towards the young man, his hand quickly moving to the gun at his side, prepared to defend his life if necessary. "Hello," he replied, tightening his grip on his revolver.

"Are you in charge?"

"Yes, I am. I'm Jethro Delaney. What can I do for you?" His voice remained cool and unfriendly.

"I'm Cassidy Eldridge, I'm Max Weber's nephew," Cassidy said. He noticed the minute the wagon master heard his uncle's name, he relaxed, as he realized he wasn't a threat to the wagon train. "I was hoping to run into him on his way west, but I guess I missed him."

"Max is usually about two or three days behind me. If you aren't in a hurry, you could wait for him in the next town as he should be arriving in a day or so."

"Thanks, is it okay if ride with your group until we get there."

"Yes, of course you're welcome to travel with us. An extra gun is always appreciated."

"Thank you. Do you mind if I just ride along side of your wagon?"

"Not at all, as it will give us time to become acquainted. How far are you headed?" he asked.

"For now, I'm going to Kansas City. Once there, and I finish my business, my plans may change."

As the wagon train continued with its westward journey, Jethro started venting to the young man about this trip's occupants. He began by enlightening Cassidy of his worries about the two pregnant women, as well as the three single women causing him too many headaches to keep track of in his old age.

Jethro went on to say he was glad he hadn't ever married, and then worried if he'd accidently insulted Cassidy with his statement. When he asked if he was married, Cassidy replied he was looking, but hadn't found the *right* woman yet.

When Jethro asked him if he wanted one of the females that were on this wagon train, he simply laughed. When Cassidy told him he didn't want a woman who was a troublemaker, Jethro chuckled, wishing him luck with finding such a woman.

As they made camp that night, Faith and Florence watched the new man ride passed them, both thinking he would soon be their husband.

"There goes my new husband," Florence told her sister.

"I don't think so," Faith said, her hand clinched at her side.

"I saw him first."

"That may be true, but I'm older, so I should get the first chance at meeting him." Faith demanded, smiling at her sister. Yes, she was older, but since they'd been born just five minutes part, that didn't make much of a difference. "I know, we'll let Sam meet him first," she said, as Sam walk passed them to do the family wash in the nearby creek.

Florence sniggered at her sister's comment.

Sam was soon forgotten as the two girls followed the man until he stopped to make his bed for the night. Soon they had his attention.

"Hello," Cassidy said to the two giggling girls. "I'm Cassidy Eldridge."

"I'm Florence Combs, and this is my *older* sister, Faith," she said, stressing the word *older* for the man's benefit.

He remembered their names from Jethro and knew these two women were trouble. He would be friendly, and then make a quick getaway. "It's nice to meet you both."

"Are you going to Oregon with us?"

"No, just going as far as Kansas City." When Cassidy caught some movement out of the corner of his eye, he turned and saw a boy coming towards them carrying a bundle of wet clothes clutched tightly against his chest.

As the boy passed, he intensely ogled Cassidy with a pair of gorgeous blue eyes, but didn't speak to him or the two women. Cassidy was surprised by the look, as the boy's bold stare made him uncomfortable, as it was the same kind of look women usually gave him.

"Well look what we have here. If it isn't Sam, one of the Tyson brothers doing the wash," Faith chimed loudly.

Both of the girls laughed, which confused Cassidy. He saw Sam give the girls a dirty look, but didn't respond, as he continued on his way. He wondered what was going on between the two girls and the young boy, but he didn't say anything to them, deciding to ask Jethro about it the next time he saw him.

Samantha fought back the tears of humiliation at their taunt of calling her a boy, especially since they were the cause of her short hair. She'd been surprised to see a good-looking stranger with them, and wondered who he was and what he was doing here. How she wished she still had her long beautiful hair, then maybe the young man wouldn't be looking at her as if she was some sort of freak of nature.

Then she frowned, knowing that even if she still had her hair, he probably wouldn't have given her a second look. She had overheard her brothers talking enough times to know most men like large breasted women. She wasn't flat chested by any means, but she definitely didn't have a bust like Faith and Florence. She hurried on her way, as before she could start the family's dinner, she had clothes to hang on the clothesline so they could start to dry.

Cassidy said goodbye to the two women and returned to Jethro's wagon to ask about the young boy with the beautiful blue eyes. When he arrived, the wagon master wasn't there, instead, there was a different young woman standing there.

Sam was quickly forgotten, as Cassidy had a new problem. At first glance the girl appeared to be shy, but as he studied her, he realized she was trouble, as she had sexually experience written all over her face. Since he had already met the two Combs sisters, he figured this must be Charissa Colligan, another of the wagon train's troublemakers. Jethro told him he didn't know why, but it seemed to him she was trying to get all the single men of the train in bed with her, including him.

"Hello, I'm Charissa Colligan," she said, thinking this young man was even better looking than either of the Tyson brothers. Now all she had to do was to get him to make love to her, and then he would be hers.

"It's nice to meet you. I'm Cassidy Eldridge," he said. When the woman continued to stand there staring at him, he became nervous. "Was there something you wanted?" he asked, hoping she would leave without causing a scene.

"I was wondering if you like to go for a stroll with me."

"I'm sorry, but I can't as I promised Jethro, I would help with the night watch. I'm going to find a quiet place to grab a few winks before I need to report for my shift." He thought she would say good night and be on her way, but instead he was surprised by her next words.

"I'm willing to help you find a quiet spot, but I doubt you'll get much rest," she cooed at him as she wrapped her hand around his wrist and brought his hand to her breast.

He was so scandalized by her actions; it took a few seconds before he could find his tongue. "Thank you for your kind offer, but I'm not interested," he said, quickly stepping out of her grip.

"I think you're rude," she said angrily. "I thought we could be friends, but I guess not," she replied through clinched teeth.

The speed in which her anger had burst from her lips had stunned him. "We can be friends. I just don't need a lover."

"It's your loss," Charissa said crossly, and then she stomped off into the night, not once looking back at him.

As he watched her storm away, he smiled, thinking his quick actions had just saved himself from a bad situation.

The day had been an extremely warm day, one that left Samantha feeling hot and sweaty. After she had laid out the laundry, she decided to take a bath in the creek to cool off. She asked Drew to come with her and be her watchdog while she bathed, as she didn't want Earl Vorbeck to surprise her while she was naked and unable to protect herself from his attention.

Drew followed her and when they reached the creek bed, he sat down on a rock, turning his back to his sister. "Sam, make it quick. I want to make sure everything is ready for us to leave tomorrow morning."

"Drew, I know the real reason you want to get back to camp, so why not just admit it."

"Fine, I want to talk to Cassidy. I heard Jethro saying he was fast with a gun and I wanted him to give me some tips."

"I'll hurry." Samantha moved to a small cove that was out of the creek's swift current and began to bath. Knowing her brother was anxious to find Cassidy, she hurried, and when she was ready to get out of the creek, she told Drew to go on.

As she put her feet on the muddy bottom and started for the bank, she heard a sound to her left. Afraid Earl had found her, she looked up, and was surprised to see Cassidy standing there watching her. "How long have you been watching me?" she asked him nervously.

"I just got here." Now that he was here with the young boy, he wished he hadn't come.

She watched in dismay as he sat down on the bank as if he planned to stay awhile. "What do you think you're doing?" she asked anxiously.

"Just making sure you don't drown."

"Well, you can see I'm getting out, so I don't need you watching over me."

"I wanted to talk to you without the entire train listening to our conversation."

"Well, say what you came to say and get out of here."

He didn't understand the boy's insistence that he leave. "Since I'm already here, I might as well take my bath too."

She watched in horror as he began to take off his boots. "Drew just left here to go find you. Why don't you go find my brother before your bath?"

"Ok, but I'm still going to wait until you're out as I would hate for you to drown as soon as I turn my back," he said jokingly.

"I rather you didn't wait for me. I don't have any clothes on."

"You don't have anything I haven't seen before," he taunted. He didn't know why he simply didn't leave and come back after the boy had time to put his clothes back on, but something seemed to prevent him from doing so.

When Cassidy didn't move, she realized he wasn't going to leave until she was out of the creek. Knowing she couldn't stay in the water all night, that left nothing else for her to do but to leave the water as he watched her. "Fine, then have it your way," she said angrily. "When my brothers hear about this, you can bet they won't be happy with you."

"Why should they care if I see you naked?" But as soon as her pear-shaped breasts came out of the water, he knew why Sam's brothers would be angry with him. "Good God, you're a woman!" he exclaimed as he jumped up and swiftly turned his back to her. As he looked towards the camp, all he could see in his mind was her beautiful perky breasts, with her nipples puckered from the cool air that had hit them. It had been a fast glance, but it was now burnt into his memory.

"Of course, I am. What did you think I was?" she asked, her feelings hurt by his words.

"I thought you were a boy."

Tears quickly formed, hurt at knowing he had thought she was a boy all the while she'd been day dreaming, he would ask her to marry him. "I might not be in the same category as some of the other females on the wagon train, but I'm still a woman."

"I see that now." He heard her step out of the water and walk to where her clothes must have been.

"What did you want to talk to me about?" she asked him as she hurriedly dressed.

"It doesn't matter now," he said, hoping she didn't ask any more questions.

"Tell me anyway."

He cringed, knowing he had to be truthful with her. "I came down here to ask you to stop watching me."

"I apologize for staring at you. I promise to keep my eyes down whenever you're around."

He didn't know what to say to her, knowing his comment had hurt her. "Why do Faith and Florence call you Sam?"

"My name is Samantha. My family and friends call me Sam for short, but the way Faith and Florence say it, it's meant to be spiteful."

Now that Cassidy knew she was a woman, he understood that even while thinking he was a boy, his mind must have sensed she was a woman all along. Now he understood why he'd been fascinated by her, as she was too beautiful to be a male. "Why haven't I ever seen you in a dress? Why is your hair cut so short?"

"Would you believe on our first night with the wagon train, some animal crawled to where I was sleeping under our wagon and cut off all my hair? That same critter also got into my wagon and stole the *only* two dresses I owned?"

"Faith and Florence?"

"Yes. Of course, they denied it. But everyone knew who was guilty of the crime. When they saw my brothers, they thought I was a rival for their attention, so they decided to take me out of the running, but instead it did just the opposite." She finished dressing and came out behind the bush. "You can turn around now."

He turned to face her and grimaced, as his desire for the young woman before him was so strong that he clinched his hands into a fist to prevent from grabbing her and pulling her into his arms. "Did they get into trouble?"

"Of course not! Their father said his daughters wouldn't ever do something that cruel to another person. Now I just make sure I stay away from them."

"Now that you're out, I'll go look for your brother," he said hurriedly when the urge to pull her into his arms became unbearable and was gone before she could respond.

The next day started with Jethro asking Cassidy if he could ride to the end of the train to make sure everyone was still with them. With Andrea's baby due any day, he didn't want them to fall too far behind if she went into labor. No matter what he told Boone, Jethro knew he couldn't leave them behind and take the chance of some misfortune befalling them. So, he'd decided they would stop when the woman went into labor.

When Jethro asked Cassidy if he would ride at the end of the train, and he accepted the man's request. As he traveled to the last wagon, he rode by the Combs's wagon in a quick trot without looking over at them, hoping to get by before either of the sisters could call out to him. Not wanting to give Charissa any encouragement either, Cassidy rode passed the next wagon the same as he had the one before.

When he came upon the next wagon, he saw the woman from last night and was greatly disappointed when she quickly dropped her eyes, but then he had been the one who had requested her not to stare at him any longer.

When Cassidy reached the end of the train, he was happy to see all the wagons were accounted for, including Boone and Andrea Farrell. As he turned his horse around, he decided to stay where he was, as this way he wouldn't have to go pass the two giggling girls, the woman who'd proposition him last night, nor the young woman who he couldn't keep off his mind.

Samantha dropped her eyes to prevent herself from staring at Cassidy, which had been extremely hard for her to do, as she was very attracted to him. She bet if he ever kissed her, he would make her body sing and her spirit soar, as just looking at him seemed to cause her heart to pulsate faster in her chest. He rode pass instead of acknowledging her, taking her heart with him. Later that night as she lay on her pallet in the hot wagon, her eyes closed and she began dreaming of Cassidy proposing. She smiled in her sleep, as in her dream, they lived happily ever after.

Day after day, as the wagon train moved closer to Boonville, Gerard Stolte became better acquainted with the Tyson brothers, finding they were good hard working honest men, and their sister was great with the children. He talked it over with Esther, and they decided to ask the three Tysons to move to Fayette with them to help them with their new ranch.

When Gerard went to find the Tyson family, he came across Drew first. "Drew, could I talk to you and your family for a few minutes," he asked, not giving the young man even a hint of what he may want with the three of them.

Drew looked at him in puzzlement. "Is something wrong?"

"No, I just wanted to talk about your future."

"I'll go find the rest of my family and meet you back at your wagon."

As Drew and his family walked back to Gerard's wagon, they discussed what Mr. Stolte could possibly want to talk to them about, but none of them had any idea. When they reached the Stolte wagon, they stopped at the end of their wagon.

"Gerard, we're here," Drew called out.

Gerard poked his head out, smiling at the three nervous faces as he climbed down. "I didn't mean to scare you. I just wanted to offer your family a job at our ranch in Fayette."

The Tysons so surprised by his proposition were speechless.

When they didn't respond, Gerard quickly explained why he wanted them to come to his ranch. "Esther and I have watched how hard you all have worked during this trip and Samantha is so wonderful with our children. While you two help us with the ranch, Samantha would help Esther with the house, and the children for a few months, but after that, Samantha is free to do whatever she wants. I know your family has plans to go to California, but we would love for you to come with us and be part of our family."

"I don't know what to say." Drew looked at Corey and Samantha before responding further. "Let us discuss it and then we'll get back to you."

"Wait, before you go, I want you to know that after you have helped us get our place up and running, we're giving your family one hundred acres. There aren't any strings attached to this proposal and the land would be completely yours to do with whatever you wanted."

"You got to be kidding," Corey uttered, shocked by the-too-good-to-be true offer.

"No, I'm not kidding. There is a house already on the property, but I'm not sure what condition it may be in. Not only that, but we need help with buying cattle, making sure all the fences are in good repair, and then whatever needs done on a regular basis. Your family will do a great job of helping us, and so we want to repay you."

The three siblings step away before Corey spoke. "Drew, I don't know about you or Sam, but I think we should take Gerard's offer."

Samantha nodded. "I think Corey's right. We haven't any idea of what we'll find in California, and besides, at least this way we know we'll be getting some land. Calvin and Daisy are wonderful children, I don't mind helping with them or with the house," she added, glad their time with Ruth Vorbeck, the Combs sisters, and Charissa Colligan was almost over, thank goodness.

"Okay, it's a unanimous decision," Drew said excitedly.

The threesome returned to Gerard. "Gerard, my family has decided to come with you," Drew told him

"How wonderful." Gerard turned towards the wagon. "Esther come out here," he called happily.

Esther hurried out of the back of the wagon. "They've accepted our proposition?"

"Yes, we're going to Fayette with you," Samantha said excitedly.

"That's wonderful." Esther climbed down and ran over to her. "You don't mind helping me with the children?"

"Of course not, they're lovely well-behaved children. They could give Faith and Florence lessons on manners."

Everyone laughed.

"Do you mind doing all the housework for a few months?" she asked nervously.

Samantha looked at her in bewilderment. "Esther, what's going here? I have the feeling there is something you aren't telling us." Samantha grabbed hold of Esther's hands. "Why won't you be doing any of your housework? Are you sick?"

"We're going to have another baby."

Samantha screamed and hugged Esther to her. "That's wonderful news. You must be ecstatic."

"We are, but this is an unexpected pregnancy. I'm not as young as I was with the first two, so I don't want to overdo it and risk losing the baby."

It was late by the time the Tyson family returned to their wagon, the two brothers still discussing what they wanted to do once they got their land. When Samantha saw Cassidy walking towards them, she tried to keep her eyes away from him, but knowing their time together was almost over, she couldn't stop staring at him. She was disappointed he hadn't ever taken an interest in her, but with her not being a beauty; she understood why he didn't find her attractive.

She wanted to talk to him since that night beside the creek, but she lacked the courage or the confidence, so instead, she just ogled him with longing behind his back. How she wished he were going to Fayette too, as then maybe, they could fall in love and get married. She smiled at the fantasy of someday marrying the handsome man.

Cassidy hurried by the Tyson family, giving them a nod in an acknowledgment as he passed. He wanted to be friendly, but not so sociable the young girl would think he was interested in her, as she was too young for him. Since he couldn't fight his obsession of the young woman, Cassidy decided when they reached the next town he would stay there until his uncle's train arrived.

Just before noon on Wednesday, they crossed the Missouri River. Since Jethro wanted to let everyone, including the animals, time to recuperate after the grueling trip across the river, they started setting up camp just outside of Boonville's city limits. Tonight, was the last night the whole group would be together, as the families going to Fayette would be leaving first thing in the morning for their final day of travel.

But Felix Atwood had other plans, tired of sleeping in the wagon for another night; he wanted to spend the night in a hotel. His plans were to have a stiff drink and then find a loose woman for a sex-filled night, as he hadn't had a woman since starting their trip.

When Charissa had heard the Atwoods were spending the night in town, she begged her father into allowing them to do the same. Before they left for town, Jethro told Brock they were leaving at seven the next morning, with or without them. Brock turning towards Jillian, his eyes cold and hard, informed his daughter if they weren't back at camp before seven, there would be hell to pay.

Since they wouldn't be there for the last night with the others, Jillian went to find Samantha to tell her friend that they were going to spend the night in town. When Jillian found out Samantha would be gone when she returned, she cried, as she thought she and her new friend had another one hundred miles before they had to part. Samantha felt bad for her friend, telling her they could write each other, and someday maybe they could see each other again.

CHAPTER FOUR
Samantha & Cassidy

"Cassidy," Sam called to him.

"What?" he asked.

"I wanted to say good-bye to you."

Her statement got him off guard, as last he knew they were going on with the wagon train. "What are you talking about?" he asked, with a confused look.

"We're leaving the train in the morning."

"I thought you were going to California?" Even though he thought she was too young for him, he wasn't ready to lose her, especially since he realized she was the woman he wanted to marry.

"We were, but my brothers have accepted a job with Gerard Stolte, so we're going to his place in Fayette to work on his cattle ranch."

Realizing he had to do something to keep her in his life, he reached out and pulled her into his arms. Then before she could do anything to prevent it, Cassidy brought his lips to hers.

The shock he received at their first contact surprised him, but he didn't stop kissing her, as he was enjoying it too much. When he finally removed his lips from hers, he moved slightly away and looked into her eyes. "Will you marry me?" he whispered softly.

She just stared at him, her eyes wide with disbelief. Never in her wildest dreams did she actually think he would ever propose marriage to her, especially since she looked like a boy.

"Tell me to get lost or that you'll be my wife, but for the love of God, say something."

"I'm a bit flabbergasted by your sudden proposal. You've never indicated you were interested."

"I tried not to be interested, as I think you're too young for me, but I can't stand the thought of never seeing you again."

"I'm eighteen," she said. How old did you think I was?"

He was surprised, as she was older than he thought. "Eighteen?" he asked. "I thought you were closer to sixteen."

"Do you still think I'm too young for you?"

"No, you're just right."

"Thank you, I think. How old are you?"

"I turned twenty-two last week." He grinned at her. "So, what's your answer?"

Tears suddenly filled her eyes as she thought of leaving her brothers. She wanted to say yes to this man's proposal, but she didn't want to leave the only family she had left. Why did she have to choose between Cassidy and her brothers?

"Well? What is it going to be? Will you marry me?" He didn't like that she just stood there with tear-filled eyes.

She smiled a weak grin at him. "I'm sorry. I would love to accept your marriage proposal, but I don't want to leave my brothers."

He smiled at her as he took hold of her hand. "I'm not asking you to give up your brothers. Tomorrow we can get married in Boonville, then start our life together near your brothers, as I'm sure I can find some work in Fayette."

"You're willing to do that for me?" she asked tearfully.

"I'll do anything to make you, my wife."

A tear dropped down her cheek, as she was touched, he was willing to give up his own plans in order to marry her. "I like the sound of that."

His lips returned to hers, and this time the kiss was longer. When he thought he couldn't stop himself from taking her in the grass, he drew away from her as his sexually desire for her soared through him.

"I guess we should find your brothers and tell them our news," he said with a nervous laugh.

Samantha looked at him. "You're afraid they'll say you can't marry me?"

"I'm not going to ask. I'm going to tell them we're going to be married."

Samantha laughed. "Brave man."

Cassidy frowned at her. "You think they'll say we can't be married?"

"Cassidy, I'm old enough to make that decision for myself." She smiled at him. "Come on, let's get this over with," she said, taking hold of his hand.

Cassidy and Samantha walked towards their wagons to find her brothers. When Faith and Florence saw them together, they frowned, each assuming the couple was just returning from a romantic tryst in the woods. What they didn't understand was how Cassidy found Samantha more attractive than they were with her hair chopped off like a boy's.

Faith told her sister it didn't really matter, as Sam would be leaving in the morning with her brothers and then they would have Cassidy to themselves. They both smiled at the thought of crawling into his bedroll with him.

When the lovebirds saw Drew and Corey sitting by the fire with the remaining people of the train, they went to join them.

Cassidy looked down at the two men. "Could I talk to you privately over by your wagon?" he asked nervously.

The two brothers looked at each other and then back at their sister and the man holding her hand.

"Is something wrong?" Drew asked, carefully watching his sister's expression, unsure what to think when he saw her nervous smile.

"No, there isn't anything wrong," she insisted.

Both men followed the couple to their wagon.

Cassidy stopped and turned to face Samantha's brothers. "I wanted you to know I've asked your sister to marry me and she said yes. We plan to get married tomorrow before you leave for Fayette."

"What?" Drew sputtered with surprise, then quickly looked over at his sister. He wanted to say she couldn't marry this man, but he wouldn't, as he didn't have the right to prevent her from marrying the man she wanted. And by her smile, he knew Cassidy was the man she wanted. "You hardly even know each other," he said, hoping Sam would tell him she would wait a few months until they'd gotten to know each other better.

"It was love at first sight," Cassidy told Samantha's brother.

Samantha tightened her lips to prevent from smiling, as she knew he once thought she was boy. "Yes, it was."

Corey wasn't surprised by this announcement, as he'd been watching his sister since Cassidy had joined the wagon train. "That's wonderful," he responded with a large grin of his own. "I'm happy for you," he said, giving her a quick hug.

Samantha hugged each of her brothers. "Thanks guys." She turned to Cassidy. "Now that wasn't so bad, was it?"

He laughed a nervous chuckle. "Of course not, it was a piece of cake."

Corey reached his hand out to Cassidy. "Congratulations. You've made a great choice for a wife, as we think Samantha is a wonderful woman."

"Sam, you were supposed to help Mrs. Stolte until the baby came." Drew stated, hoping it would change his sister's mind about getting married as he was already missing her. "Once you're married, where you're going to live?"

"Your sister wants to stay near you two, so we're going to Fayette with you. Since I can work anywhere, I told her it was fine with me. I'd feel better if I knew for sure I had a way to support your sister and provide her a home, but we aren't going to wait to get married. We'll live in the wagon if we have to," Cassidy said stubbornly.

Corey touched Sam's arm. "You didn't tell him?"

"I've been in a state of shock since he kissed me." Samantha quickly covered her mouth with her hand, blushing at admitting to her brothers that there had been a kiss between them.

"Sam, you're a grown woman. I would hope you've kissed the man you're about to marry at least once before you tie the knot, as you would hate to find out after the wedding that's he's a terrible kisser," Corey teased.

Cassidy took hold of Samantha hand. "What haven't you told me?" His eyes were full of worry, unsure what she had to tell him.

"It isn't anything bad." She looked away, glancing at both of her brothers before looking back at Cassidy. "After helping the Stoltes get their place up and running, they're giving us one hundred acres to split between the three of us to do whatever we want."

"That's great. Maybe it would be best if we waited to get married until after you get your land."

Samantha frowned at his comment. "I don't want to wait. I want to marry you as soon as possible as I haven't thought of anything but becoming your wife since the first day I saw you," she told him, then looked away as she felt the warmth of embarrassment fill her cheeks.

His face brightened. "Really?" he said, as he put hand under her chin and moved her head so her eyes looked into his.

She smiled a sweet grin at him. "Yes, really." She planned to give him a quick kiss on the lips, but once her lips touched his, she was lost once again in the euphoria of his kiss. The kiss continued, that is, until a clearing of someone's throat behind her made her jump away. "Oh."

"Now I understand what she meant about his kiss," Drew teased, happy his sister had found love.

"It looked like a wonderful kiss," Corey replied in a dreamy teasing way.

Samantha moved away from Cassidy, hitting one brother, then the other one with her fist. "You two better be nice."

"I thought we were. Corey weren't we being nice?" he asked, looking over at his brother, with an ornery grin.

"Of course, we were. We both were giving his kiss a complement," Corey said, then laughed.

"You two better behave or I won't invite you to my wedding," she said, trying to sound stern.

"Sis, you wouldn't get married without your two favorite brothers," Drew teased, then turned to Cassidy. "About supporting our sister, we would need to talk to Mr. Stolte first, but he'll probably agree to hire t Cassidy to work on his ranch."

"I'd like that." Cassidy looked back and forth between the three other people. "Do you think you could ask him tonight?"

"You're afraid he'll say no?" Corey said to taunt him.

"Maybe he doesn't need another hand," Samantha uttered nervously.

"Sam, don't you worry your pretty head about it. Remember we're the Three Musketeers, if Mr. Stolte doesn't need Cassidy, he can start building our new home. No matter what, there will be some sort of work for him to do."

"Are you sure?"

"I'll go talk to him right now to put your mind to rest."

"Thank you."

"Cassidy, do you know anything ranching?" Drew thought to ask before he left to find Mr. Stolte.

"Yes, my family had a cattle ranch, but I sold it after my parents died."

"That's good to know. Come on Corey; let's go talk to our new boss about our soon to be brother-in-law. You two be good while we're gone," he teased, wiggling his eyebrows at his sister.

Samantha watching her brothers intensely as they walked towards the Stoltes' wagon, jumped when Cassidy touched her hand. "What?"

"Are your brother always like that?"

"Like what?" she asked, her eyes showing her confusion.

"Are they always taunting you?"

"Not always. It was very hard on both of them when our parents died. Suddenly Drew had to be both father and mother to us, while still trying to be our brother. When it came to make the decision to sell our place and move westward, we decided as a family."

"Do you think they could adopt me and make me their brother?"

She smiled at him. "After we're married, you'll be their brother-in-law, which makes you family."

Cassidy took hold of her hand. "I like the sound of that." But before he could pull her into his arms and kiss her, he heard Drew and Corey returning. "Here comes the verdict."

"That was fast. It mustn't be good news for them to be back so quickly." She bit her lip as she waited for her brothers to rejoin them. "Well, what did Mr. Stolte say?"

"He said he would be able to use Cassidy as there will be plenty of work for all of us. With an extra man helping, we should be able to get his place up and going weeks earlier than he planned." Drew looked over at his sister. "When his house is finished, we'll start on a house for us all to share."

"Since you're getting married, we decided you should get the first house," Corey told her.

Drew frowned at his brother for spoiling his news. "Thanks Corey."

"Sorry, I couldn't help myself, and when we have more money, we'll start on a house for the two of us."

"Sounds good, but I want it to be fair," Samantha told her brothers.

"It will be," Drew assured her.

"Once we get to the ranch and know where our share of the land will be, we can make plans where to put the first house," Drew said, looking at his siblings. "Now that's settled, I've been meaning to ask you to show me how fast you can draw," he said to Cassidy.

"I think I'd rather wait until after we've had our wedding night, as I would hate to accidentally be shot and miss my own honeymoon," Cassidy said jokingly.

Samantha blushed at his words and her brothers snickered at his comment.

Cassidy quickly turned to Samantha. "My apologies that was a crude comment to say in front of you."

"Your apologies are accepted," she replied with a smile, as she was already dreaming of her wedding night with this man beside her.

Drew and Corey walked away from the young couple, and when they were out of hearing, Drew stopped and looked over at his brother. "Do you believe in love at first sight?"

"No, I don't. I know Mother use to talk about how it happened to her when she met Father, but I don't believe it exists."

"I think it's something women just made up. I doubt I'll ever find a woman I'll want to marry just seconds after meeting her."

"I'm with you brother."

CHAPTER FIVE
Gwen & Tucker

As the Colligans and Atwoods headed into town to spend the night, the rest of the wagon train began to fix their evening meal. Brock and his daughters rode on Felix's wagon gate for the short distance into town, leaving their wagon sitting where they parked it earlier that afternoon.

Since Felix and Gwen wouldn't be returning to the camp, but heading out to their new home in the morning, the Colligans would have to walk back to camp. Charissa complained so loudly about having to do any sort of physical labor that her father said he would hire someone to drive her back to camp.

As Brock and Felix checked into the hotel, Gwen hugged Jillian goodbye. With tears in her eyes, she gave her new friend her address in Fayette, making her promise to write and Jillian said she would.

When Felix and Gwen reached their room, he opened the door for her, and Gwen went in. He said he'd be back later and then without explaining, he closed the door and left without her.

Gwen swung when she heard the door close. Standing alone in the empty room, she remained there several seconds in a daze before she could move. Then fear filled her at the thought of her husband returning to the room drunk and forcing himself on her. She turned and said a silent prayer, asking that he'd simply pass out in whatever woman's room he went to so she wouldn't have to deal with him and his sexually advances.

She opened the small bag she had with her and pulled out her nightgown. She took off her gown, then poured some water in basin, and took a sponge bath. Once she felt clean, she put on her gown and went to bed. She smiled as she rested her head on the soft pillow, as the bed felt as if she was floating on a cloud. Then she put her hands on her rounding belly, closed her eyes, and instantly fell sound asleep.

Tucker Lowery was tired from his long day of traveling, but he wanted a drink before he checked in at the hotel. He'd planned to be at his family home by now, but not one thing had gone right for his since he left Oklahoma. Therefore, instead of being at this sister's home sitting in her kitchen with her, he was stuck in Boonville, nearly thirty miles from home as darkness had made him stop for the night.

He and his sister, Krista Owens, had been born and raised in Fayette, growing up in the same house his sister still live in. Krista and her husband, Lester had lived on the family ranch, with the hope of raising a houseful of children, but then a year ago, Lester had been killed. Expect for two cowhands that worked for her, Krista was alone on the ranch. Part of the reason Tucker was moving to Fayette was he wanted to be closer to his sister; the other part was he was hoping to buy the land next to hers.

He'd tried for several years to buy the property that belonged to their elderly neighbor, but each time he made an offer, the old man refused, saying he was saving it for his granddaughter. Recently Tucker received news from his sister the old man had died. As far as he knew, the old man hadn't heard from his family for the past ten years, so he doubted the granddaughter would want the property.

Once he reached Fayette, he was going to speak with the man's solicitor and offer to buy the place. If he were turned down again, he would live with his sister until he found another place to buy, as he planned to make his home near his sister.

Tucker stepped into the saloon and went to the bar to order a drink. After he sat down at a nearby table, he immediately noticed a middle-aged man who was causing trouble at the next table. Suddenly the man stood, pulled out his gun, and aimed it straight at Tucker's head.

"She's my wife, you can't have her," he yelled, then he pulled the trigger rapidly at Tucker's head.

The man's first bullet missed Tucker by bare inches, and the second bullet flew into his hat, knocking it onto the floor. While ducking to protect himself from the next bullet, Tucker responded by drawing his gun and shooting at the man, then the room became quiet, as the shooter now lay dead on the floor.

"Are you hurt?" a man asked Tucker as he helped him up off the floor.

"No, I'm fine."

"He talked as if you were interested in his wife," the man accused him.

"I just rode into town five minutes ago. I don't know him or his wife. Is he okay?"

"You killed him, but I wouldn't worry about it. I'm sure his wife is probably better off without him," the man replied thoughtlessly.

"I guess I better go find his wife and tell her about her husband," he said as he looked down at the dead man. "Do you know who he was?"

"He said his name was Felix Atwood."

"Do you want me to go tell the wife?" asked a second man who'd just come up to them.

Tucker studied the new man beside him. "Why would you tell her?"

"I'm Jack Bennett, the sheriff of this town," he said. "I'm not on duty tonight, so I'm not wearing my badge," he added when he noticed Tucker looking at his vest for his star.

"Thanks for offering, but I think I should be the one to tell her."

"Have it your way, but if you don't mind, I'll come with you just in case she has any questions."

"Suit yourself. Do you know where they live?"

"From what I overheard from his conversation, he and his wife had been with a wagon train. They were staying at the hotel so they could sleep on a soft bed before continuing with the rest of their journey," replied the first man.

"I don't blame them. That's where I wish I was."

"You and me both," replied the sheriff.

When the two men arrived at the hotel, Jack asked the hotel clerk which room the Atwoods were staying. A few minutes later, the two men were at Gwen's door and Tucker knocked lightly on it.

Gwen jerked awake when she heard the knock at her hotel door, startled at the sound of Felix knocking at the door. She had turned down the lantern before she had gone to bed, leaving just enough light so Felix could find his way to bed when or if he came back to the room. She got out of bed and hurried to the door before her husband could knock again.

When she opened it, she gasped at the sight of two strangers standing at her door. Thinking they wanted to do her harm, she quickly slammed the door closed in their face and locked it.

The two men exchanged puzzled looks. "What was that all about?" Tucker asked the sheriff.

"Maybe seeing two men at this time of night scared her."

Tucker nodded. "I didn't think anything about it, as I had my mind on telling her about her husband, not how our appearance may startle her." He turned back to the door. "Mrs. Atwood, I need to talk to you regarding your husband," Tucker called.

"What about him?" she asked through the closed door.

"Ma'am, I'd rather not talk to you while standing out in the hall."

"I don't care. I don't know you." She was prepared to scream if need be as she knew there wasn't any way she could fight them if they were there to assault her.

"Ma'am, my name is Tucker Lowery. I'm with Jack Bennett, the sheriff of Boonville, and we need to talk privately with you."

The man's name didn't register with her, as she was too nervous finding two men at her door late at night to comprehend his name from her memory.

"Let me put on my robe."

After putting on her robe, Gwen reopened the door to her guests. Her hand automatically went to her enlarged belly in a protective move as she looked at the two men.

Tucker's eyes followed her hand as it went to her stomach. "Damn," he swore as he got his first glimpse of her pending motherhood. He'd been expecting to see a woman in her late forties or early fifty's, definitely not this beautiful young pregnant woman. How Tucker wished this ordeal were over.

"Excuse me?" she replied, shocked by the man's language.

"I apologize for my language, Mrs. Atwood," Tucker replied, embarrassed by his vulgarity. "We need to speak privately with you, and what we have to say shouldn't be discussed in the hallway," Tucker muttered, unhappy at having to tell this young woman, she was now a widow thanks to him.

"Fine." She stepped back to allow the two men to enter. When Tucker started to shut the door behind them, she put her hand out to stop him. "I'd prefer if you kept the door open, for if my husband should return to our room, he wouldn't be happy to find two strange men in it with me."

"Yes, ma'am," Tucker mumbled over the knot growing in his throat. Now that he'd seen her and her condition, he wasn't sure if he would be able to tell her what he'd done.

Jack waited impatiently for the young man to tell her his dreadful news, but he just stood there staring at her. When the other man didn't speak to her, he nudged him with his elbow. "Tell her."

"Mrs. Atwood, I'm sorry to inform you, but your husband is . . .," He looked at the sheriff, then back to her.

"Yes, what about him?" She just wanted him to say what he had to say and leave. Hopefully, they would be gone before Felix could return. If he caught two young good-looking men in her room, she knew he would beat her, no matter why they were there.

"I'm afraid he's dead," Tucker stated hurriedly.

"What?" Her voice squeaked, her eyes fluttered, and then she began falling towards the floor.

Tucker quickly reached out and grabbed hold of her before she could hit the floor and was quite shocked at the electricity that shot through him on contact. Not knowing what else to do, he picked her up and quickly laid her on top of her bed, then took a step back. Looking down at her, he wanted to touch her again to see if the spark was still there, but knew he couldn't, especially with the sheriff watching him.

"Damn, I hadn't any idea she was expecting a baby. I hated to be the one to tell her about her husband, but since I was the one who killed him, I felt it was my responsibility." As Tucker stared down at the pregnant woman, he suddenly made a life changing decision. Since he couldn't with good consciousness leave her alone to defend for herself, as soon as she woke, he would to propose marriage to her.

"Mr. Lowery, you didn't have a choice, as it was either you or him. If you want, I'll stay with her until she wakes up."

"No. I've made a decision and I need to talk to her about it.

"What kind of decision?" the sheriff asked, puzzled by the man's comment.

"She's a widow because of me," he started, but before he could say anymore, Gwen's eyes began to flutter open.

The two men took a step back from the bed and tried not to stare at her as she began to awaken.

Gwen opened her eyes. When she looked around the room, the first person she saw was the handsome man who had told her about Felix. When she realized she was lying on the bed, she quickly sat up, then wobbled as the room swam before her eyes.

Quickly a pair of strong hands was on her arms to steady her, and then just as abruptly as they came, they were gone. Gwen stared at the man, surprised by electrical sensation she'd felt by his simple touch.

"I'm sorry about your husband."

"Do you know what happened?" She really didn't care, but she thought she should at least pretend to these men that she did.

Tucker looked at the sheriff and then back at her. "There was an incident in the bar. Your husband suddenly pulled out his gun, aimed it at me, and shouted, 'You can't have her'. When he shot at me repeatedly, I responded by . . .," he started, then he looked down at his feet. "I'm sorry, I killed your husband."

"Don't worry about it."

His eyes shot up to her face, stunned by her cold response.

"Before you decide to live out the rest of your life feeling guilty about killing my husband, I must tell you he wasn't a nice man. The world is definitely a better place without Felix Atwood."

He realized he shouldn't judge her, as he didn't know what kind of life she'd had with her husband. "Is there anything I can do for you?" He wanted to initiate his proposition to her now, but didn't want the sheriff to be present when he did so.

"I need to get to Fayette, but don't know the way. Do you know someone who would be willing to take me?" she asked the two men.

"Mrs. Atwood, I'll be honored to take you wherever you what to go."

"Thank you, but I wouldn't want you to go out of your way because of me. I'm sure I can find someone else to take me."

"I'm going to Fayette to visit my sister and to see into a business matter, I assure you, it won't be out of my way at all."

"Thank you, Mister . . ." She looked at him.

"Tucker Lowery, ma'am."

Gwen looked at him, confused to why his name seemed familiar to her. Then she realized he had introduced himself when she had first opened the door, and she must have forgotten it when he told her about Felix. As how else would his name seem familiar to her?

"Where's Felix's body now?"

"He's been taken to the undertaker. I could take you there in the morning if you want," Jack responded.

"Maybe you could just handle his burial for me?" she hesitantly asked the sheriff.

"You don't want to do it yourself?" he asked her, confused by her comment.

"I know you must think terrible of me, but Felix was a horrible man and now that he's dead, I don't want to have any more to do with him." She blushed at her cold comment, as she didn't want these men to think badly of her.

Jack acknowledged her remark with a nod. "I'll be happy to handle it for you."

"Thank you. If you can let me know the expense of his burial, I'll make sure the undertaker is paid."

"Ma'am, if I may, I would like to pay for your husband's interment," Tucker told her.

"Thank you, but I wouldn't feel right letting you pay for it."

"Maybe you two could discuss this in the morning. It's late and we should be going so you could get some rest," Jack told her. "If you should need anything, anything at all, please don't hesitate to stop by my office," he told her.

"Thank you, Sheriff. I'll stop by your office before I leave town tomorrow."

"Until then," he said as he tilted his hat at her, "good night."

"Good night." Gwen watched as the nervous sheriff left the room. When she noticed the other man didn't follow him, she looked over at the man named Tucker. She could tell he was anxious about something, but she couldn't figure out what it had to do with her.

"Was there something else you wanted to say to me?" She wasn't comfortable standing alone in her room with this stranger in her just her nightclothes.

"Yes, ma'am."

"What is it?" she asked tensely, afraid the man had some sort of evil intent in mind now that the sheriff was gone.

"I know I haven't a right to ask you, especially since I'm the one who took your husband's life," he started, but stopped when he lost his nerve. How could he ask her to marry the man who'd killed her husband not even thirty minutes ago?

"Ask me what?"

Tucker took off his hat and twisted his fingers in the brim. He couldn't *not* propose, as he wouldn't feel right letting her fend for herself in her condition. "Will you marry me?"

Gwen simply stared at the fretful man. "What?"

"I feel obligated to make sure you're taking care of because of your condition, and marriage is the only way I know how to do that."

She gave him a soft smile, touched by his offer. "You don't have to marry me."

"I'd be honored to have you as my wife."

She smiled at him, then leaned over and kissed his cheek.

Tucker felt himself blushing, something he never remembered doing before.

She wanted to refuse his offer, as she wasn't ready to have another man in her life, but she knew this was important to this man. Besides, she knew she couldn't run her grandfather's farm by herself, especially with a baby coming. "Sir, I would be honored to marry you."

"Really?" Tucker was completely shocked by her response.

"Yes, really."

"When?"

"Could we wait until morning?" she asked, with a faint smile on her lips.

He laughed. "Sure. Do you have a preference to where you live?"

She hated the thought of selling her grandfather's place, but she assumed this man probably already had a ranch of his own. "I have business to take care of in Fayette, but once it's been taken care of, I'm free to go anywhere," she said regretfully.

"Perfect. I must tell you if my business transpires the way I would like it to, we would be staying permanently in Fayette. Will that cause a problem for you?"

Gwen thought if they were to stay in Fayette, then maybe they could live in grandfather's home and she wouldn't have to sell it after all. She smiled at him. "No, that would work out better for me."

He had proposed to a woman and didn't even know her first name. He smiled at her. "May I know your first name?"

She giggled at his question. "My name is Gwen."

"You get some sleep. I'll be by in the morning, and then we can make plans to get married."

"I'll be ready."

"Good night, Gwen." Tucker leaned over and kissed her cheek. "Thank you for accepting my proposal."

"It was my pleasure," she said, blushing. "Good night."

She saw him to the door and once he was outside, she closed and locked it. She was smiling as she returned to her bed, thinking that tomorrow morning she would be marrying the young good-looking stranger. After she got back into bed, she closed her eyes and began thinking of Tucker Lowery, wondering about their life together once they were married.

She kept expecting fear and panic to set in at knowing she was remarrying, especially a stranger, but a soft and warm glow in heart was all she had. She fell asleep with a smile on her face, at peace at knowing she wasn't afraid of her future with Tucker, and not once did she worry if he might be like Felix.

CHAPTER SIX
Jillian & Styler

Arnie Boswell was surprised that of all people in the world, his old friend, Brock Colligan had just happened to enter the saloon. He and Brock had been close friends since they were young boys, but their friendship ended abruptly when Brock ran off with the woman Arnie was engaged to marry. Hatred filled Arnie as he watched the man who had been his friend until the day, he'd stolen the woman he loved away from him. He absentmindedly rubbed the scaring he had on the upper part of his face, near his ear, a token from a fire he was in when he was a small boy.

Arnie figured Beryl married Brock because of his wealth, something he didn't have. After he heard about their elopement, he packed up his belongings and moved away, unable to see the woman he'd loved married to his friend.

As the years passed, he thought often of Beryl, wondering what their life would have been like if they had married. His heart hardened at the thought the life Brock had stolen from him and he wanted revenge against his old friend, swearing someday he would get his chance to pay his old friend back for what he'd done.

Arnie heard from friends a year later that Brock and Beryl had a daughter, naming her Charissa. As the years passed, he'd heard different things about the family, but none of it was ever good, as the marriage wasn't a happy one. Arnie was glad, as he felt Brock deserved the bad marriage.

Shortly after their second anniversary, Beryl had been walking from the barn to the house when a bolt of lightning struck and killed her. Brock was devastated at the loss of his wife, but he kept going for the sake of their young daughter.

Arnie knew Brock remarried a few months later to Angela Wilton, a very beautiful young woman, and nine months later, she gave birth to Jillian. As the two girls got older, he heard how the older sister was cruel to the younger one, and he figured Charissa was fighting to remain their father's favorite. A couple of years later, the second wife died from pneumonia, leaving her young daughter in the care of a father who favored her older sister.

As Arnie sat there staring at Brock, an evil plot to get his revenge began to form in his mind. Since Charissa was Brock's favorite, he would kidnap her and have his way with her before sending her back home to her father. What better way to punish Brock for stealing the woman he was going to marry than to take his daughter from him and violate her.

As the revenge plot played out in his mind, Arnie decided he would keep her with him until she was heavy with his child, then he would send her home. Arnie laughed loudly at that thought, startling the other men at his table.

For his plan to work he had to get out of here before Brock could see him, as otherwise his revenge was doomed before it got started. He snuck out the back door and hurried over to the hotel to inquire if Brock's daughters were in town with him. When he arrived, the clerk had stepped away from the desk, so he simply took the opportunity to check the register for himself, ecstatic to see Charissa was in room five, and Jillian was in room seven.

He went to room five, and knocked hard on the door. When the young woman opened the door, the first thing he noticed was how beautiful she was. He smiled a wicked smile, immediately knowing he was going to enjoy ravishing her. Before she could scream, he took his fist and slammed it hard into her face, hitting her with enough force to knock her unconsciousness. He quickly grabbed her as she started downwards and threw her quickly over his shoulder. He moved to the bed and grabbed a blanket from her bed, quickly covering her body with it.

He shut her door before moving quietly down the back stairs. Wanting to be sure no one saw him with a body thrown over his shoulder; he went through the empty kitchen, skulking out into the darkness with his bundle. He threw her over his saddle before mounting behind her. Once he was settled with a good grip on his hostage, he kicked the horse into a gallop into the darkness, as he wanted to get as far away as possible before the alarm of her abduction was sounded.

They had ridden for about twenty minutes when the woman moaned as she started to regain consciousness. Realizing he didn't have much time before she would awaken, he stopped the horse, dismounted, and quickly pulled her down to the ground. With the moon lighting up the night, Arnie quickly pulled her hands in front of her and tied them together. When he was done, he tied a cloth around her mouth to prevent her from screaming and alerting anyone who may happen to be out tonight.

When Jillian woke, her eyes flew open, shocked to see she wasn't in her hotel room, but outside on the ground. She was confused to why her head hurt and when she started to move her hands, she was surprised to find them tied together.

"I'm sorry I didn't mean to hit you so hard."

She turned her head towards the voice and muttered an angry reply as she instantly recognized him as the man who had been at her door.

"If you promise not to scream, I'll take the gag out of your mouth."

When she nodded, he removed the gag.

"What do you want?" she asked through her constricted throat.

He smiled an evil smile. "What any man would want from you."

"No!" she screamed.

He hit her across the face. "Damn it, you promised you wouldn't scream." He lightly stroked his hand across her cheek. "It really doesn't matter, Charissa, as there isn't anyone out here to hear you, so don't waste your breath."

She didn't understand how this man knew of her sister or why he would want her, all she knew was that he had the wrong sister. "I'm Jillian, Charissa's my sister," she told him.

"You're lying," he shouted at her. "I checked the register and showed you were room five."

"No, I'm not lying. Since my room was larger my sister insisted, we exchanged rooms."

From what he'd heard about Charisa, he had to believe her. "It doesn't really matter. You're Brock Colligan's daughter, ain't ya?" he asked, his evil eyes staring with lust at her.

"Yes," she replied slowly. Afraid what his man planned for her; tears started down her face.

"Then you'll do for what I have planned."

She didn't understand what her father had to done to this man to cause him to want to kidnap her, but the thought was quickly forgotten, as moved her arms upward, then his body fell on top of her. Knowing instantly what was about to happen, she screamed again as she tried to fight him off. Though her hands were tied, she clasped her hands together, bent her elbows, and brought it down on his head.

The attack didn't faze him, and since he was stronger, it wasn't long before she felt cool air reached her as he pulled up her nightgown. As she continued to struggle, she felt something warm and hard touch her private woman place, then as suddenly as he was on her, his body was gone.

When she sat up, she was surprised to see a man brawling with her kidnapper. Knowing she had to get away while her kidnapper was otherwise occupied, she brought her hands to her mouth and using her teeth, she struggled to untie the rope around her hands. When the knot wouldn't budge, Jillian gave up on the rope and went to the man's horse. She tried to mount it, but the horse was too skittish for her to get her foot into the stirrup.

When she felt a set of hands on her arms, she jumped back. Knowing she couldn't let the man get hold of her again, she instantly swung her clasped hands at the person's head, but the stronger hands stopped her before she could connect with his head.

"Whoa, there little lady I'm not going to hurt you," a deep male voice said to her as he gently held her hands in his.

She looked at the man's face and suddenly sucked in her breath. Instead of the kidnapper, an extremely handsome man had hold of her.

He quickly dropped her hands and stepped away. "Are you hurt?" he asked gently, trying to keep his eyes from looking down at her nightgown.

"He raped me," she cried, falling to the ground at the horror of what had happened to her.

Skyler knelt down to her. "I'm sorry I didn't get here sooner. I tried to find you as soon as I heard your first scream, but I'm not familiar with the area so I had a hard time locating you in the dark. Let me remove the rope from your wrists."

After he untied her, Skyler gave Jillian his shirt to put on over her nightgown. He felt horrible at what the beautiful young woman had suffered at the hands of the other man and wished he'd killed the man instead of just knocking him out cold.

"Did he escape?" she asked, her eyes filled with fear as she dressed.

When he heard the panic in her voice, he wanted to embrace her, but was afraid of scaring her. "No, I knocked him out, so I still need to tie him to a tree. You stay right here while I take care of him."

"No!" she cried. "Don't leave me."

"He can't hurt you," he said, putting his arms around her as she sobbed against his shoulder.

"No man will want me now," she mumbled into his chest.

Skyler tightened his arms around her as she spoke. "Don't talk that way? No one needs to know what happened here."

Jillian couldn't understand why this man's arms seemed to be able to comfort her, but they did. She didn't know if it was the man's good looks or because he had rescued her, but she felt safe for the first time since her mother's death.

"I'm no longer a virgin. How will I explain to my future husband I was raped? What if I got pregnant by that monster?"

His arms tightened around her at her words, but when he felt a sexually urge surge through him, he quickly moved away from her. "I'm Skyler Emery," he said as he put his hand out.

She took hold of it and they shook hands. "I'm Jillian Colligan."

"Colligan? Are you related to Charissa Colligan?"

"Yes, she's my sister," she told him, confused how he would even know her sister so many miles away from their home.

Skyler was shocked by her statement as he looked at her more closely in the moonlight. "Do you look anything like her?"

"No, I don't, but then we had different mothers. Do you know her?"

"No, we haven't ever met. She knows two of my cousins."

"Do your cousins live in Charlottesville?"

"No, but that's where they met your sister."

"Lucky them," she replied sarcastically.

He wasn't sure what her comment meant, but he didn't ask her to explain. "Where were you staying when you were kidnapped?"

"I was at a hotel in Boonville. My father, my sister, and I are traveling on a wagon train to Kansas City. Because Charissa was tired of sleeping in the wagon, she talked my father into spending the night in town before continuing our trip. Otherwise, we would have spent the night in our wagon with the rest of the people on the wagon train."

Skyler nodded. "I see."

"For some reason the man thought I was my sister, but I don't know why he would want to kidnap her either. I think it had something to do with my father, but I'm not sure what that reason could be."

"Maybe we can find out why he attacked you in the morning." He took hold of her hand. "It's late so we should sleep here tonight instead of trying to travel back to Boonville in the dark. I have a bedroll you can use. I'll start a fire to help keep the wildlife away, and then I need to unsaddle the horses for the night."

"What will you sleep on if I use your bedroll?"

"Don't worry about me, I'll lay on one of the horse blankets."

Jillian nodded, then watched as he returned to the kidnapper and tied him to a nearby tree, once that was done, he took care of the horses.

As Skyler unsaddled the kidnapper's horse, he admired the young stallion, wishing the horse belonged to him, as he would make a good stud horse for his horse ranch. When he was finished with the man's horse, he took the blanket to the kidnapper and covered him with it.

When he finished taking care of his own horse, he dropped the bedroll next to Jillian, then moved away to lay out the blanket for his bed. When he looked over at her, he was surprised to see she hadn't moved from where she sat, and the bedroll was where he had dropped it.

Skyler returned to her and knelt down beside her. "Here let me help you," he said as he unrolled the bedding for her. "Now lay down and I'll cover you up." The desire to join her filled him, but he knew it wasn't going to happen. This woman didn't need to be rolling around in a bedroll with him after what she'd experience earlier tonight.

She grabbed hold of his hand. "Don't leave me. I don't want to be alone."

He sensed her fear as her grip tightened on his hand. "Let me get my blanket." He pulled his hand away, and hurried to retrieve his blanket. When he returned, he remade his bed next to hers.

She lay down next to him as close as possible without actually touching him, then turned to her side, facing away from him. As she laid there trying to relax and go to sleep, her mind kept replaying what the other man had done to her and began crying.

When Skyler heard her softly sobbing, he did the only thing he knew to do to soothe her; and that was to put his arm around her and pull her tightly against him.

She took in a deep breath and just smelling in his scent seemed to bring her comfort, the tears quit, and she fell asleep.

At five the next morning, Brock went to Charissa's room and knocked on the door, as he wanted to leave for the wagon train camp as soon as they had some breakfast. When she didn't answer his knock, he opened the door and looked inside. When he saw she wasn't there, he wondered if she was already downstairs eating. He went to Jillian's room and pounded on the door with his fist, as he wasn't going to let her be the cause of them not getting to the campsite on time.

The door opened. "What do you want?" Charissa whined. It was apparent that he'd woken her as she was still in her nightgown.

Brock's face showed his surprise when Charissa opened the door to Jillian's room.

"Charissa, what are you doing in here?"

"This room was larger than the one I was given, so I made Jillian switch with me."

"I'm going to I lose my mind."

"I'm the older sister; I should get the better room."

"I'm not going to get in to it now. Where's your sister?"

"How would I know?"

"We can't leave until we find her."

"Can't we just leave her here?"

Brock just shook his head. "You know damn well we can't leave without her. Not unless you want to marry Jacob Cobb in your sister's place," he threatened. "Now get dressed and help me find her."

An hour later, Jillian still hadn't been found which had Brock steaming, furious at her because they were running out of time to return to the wagon train before they left. Where could that girl have gone? If she ran away again, when he found her, he was going to beat her to an inch of her life.

He returned to Jillian's room, hoping to find out where she may have gone. But the only thing he saw missing was her and her nightgown, as her clothes and shoes were still in her room.

When it dawns on Brock something bad must have happened to her, a sick feeling hit him. He wasn't worried about his daughter's life, just concerned about what he was going to do about his financial situation if she didn't show up before it was time for them to leave. He frowned when he realized if Jillian didn't show up, he and Charissa would both have to get a job to pay his creditors the money due them.

That morning, when Jethro found out the Colligans hadn't returned to camp, he rode into town to check on the reason. When he stopped at the hotel and couldn't find any sign of the Colligan family, he went to the sheriff's office. He told him if he should see Brock Colligan or his daughters, tell them the wagons were leaving at seven with or without them. If they weren't back by then, they would have to wait for the next wagon train to come through or head to Kansas City on their own.

In a different part of the area, Skyler questioned the man about the kidnapping, but he refused to talk. They ate a quick breakfast of cold biscuits Skyler had in his saddlebag, and as they broke camp, Jillian kept from looking over at the kidnapper, as she was trying to forget what he had done to her last night.

After helping the man onto his horse, Skyler moved towards his own horse and help Jillian onto his horse. After she was situated, he grabbed the reins of other man's horse and mounted behind her. He tried to keep his raging hormones in order, but when his eyes looked down at her shapely exposed legs, his maleness naturally harden. He hoped she wasn't aware of his situation, because if she did, she might decide she'd rather walk. He roughly kicked his horse into a trot and they started towards Boonville.

They hadn't gone but a few miles when a snake slithered across the road, scaring Skyler's horse. When the horse reared up on his hind legs, Skyler lost hold of the other horse's reins while trying to remain in the saddle. He was unsuccessful, and as he and Jillian fell onto the hard ground, his horse took off down the road as fast he could.

Once Arnie horse's reins were free from Skyler's hand, he took advantage of the situation by leaning over and grabbing the reins. Knowing he had to get away before he could be caught again, and be sent to jail, he turned his horse towards the direction they had just come, and kicked the horse in its side. As it took off in a run, Arnie held onto the saddle horn and hoped for the best.

Because Skyler had the wind knocked out of him when Jillian had landed on his chest, it took several seconds before he could move. Once he was breathing again, he gently moved her off him and stood. He looked around for his horse, but there wasn't any sign of either horses or the other man. "Damn," he shouted loudly.

"I'm sorry," she said when she saw both of the horses was gone.

"Jillian, it wasn't your fault. I should have been keeping a better eye out for trouble. I know Buttercup doesn't like snakes."

She giggled, as she expected a man like him to have a horse with a masculine name, not something a mare would have. "Buttercup? That's the name of your horse?"

The sound of her laughter sent an electrical charge through him, which surprised him. "My cousin named him."

"Why didn't you just name him something else?"

He smiled at the memory of the day Rachelle had named his new horse. "It meant too much to her, that and I didn't want to hurt her feelings."

Jillian frowned. "How old was she when she named him?"

"She was ten."

"Were the two of you close growing up?"

"As close as any brother and sister ever were. She's now twenty and is afraid she's going to be an old maid."

"Why's that?"

"I haven't seen her for a while, but the last time I did, she was the biggest tomboy in three counties."

"Maybe she has grown out of it."

"I doubt it," he replied sadly.

"I did."

He laughed. "Somehow, I can't see you as ever being a tomboy. I bet men are knocking at your door just the same."

She looked sadly at him. "What man wants a wife that can out ride and out shoot them, and wears pants like a man?"

At her comment, he looked towards her breasts that were hidden under his shirt she wore, and what he saw, showed she was definitely all woman. Suddenly his eyes shot back upwards to hers, slightly embarrassed at where his eyes had been. His thoughts were sexual, but he knew he couldn't do anything about it, as it wasn't it the right time or place; that and most likely this woman was still a virgin. He shook his head to clear his brain of the image of making love to her. "One that is he's confident enough with himself, he won't be bothered by such things."

"I guess you're right."

"I hate to bring this up, but without having a horse, we're in trouble. Not only are we without a horse, but you aren't dressed for traveling."

"I wished I'd at least put my slippers on before I answered the door to that mad man."

He put his fingers in his mouth and let out a loud whistle.

Jillian jumped back at the sound, quickly covering her ears with her hands as she did so. "What was that for?"

"If Buttercup is nearby, he'll return to me." However, no horse showed up. "We can't just sit here and wait for help to come along, so I think we should start walking. I could carry you," he said slowly, as he was afraid what may happen if she was in his arms again.

She shook her head. "I don't think you can carry me all the way back to town, besides I'm use to walking barefoot."

"We'll start walking and maybe we'll come across help soon."

"I'm sure once my father knows I'm missing, he'll send someone to look for me."

"In the meantime," he said as he put out his hand to her, "I guess we better get going."

She took hold of his hand and smiled up at him, and then they started walking towards town. She tried to keep her mind on something that didn't pertain to the man next to her, but it was useless, his touch made her belly jump and her mind spin. Having such a dramatic response to his touch, made her wonder what it would be like to be kissed by this handsome man.

"Why were you out here in the middle of night?" she asked the young man next to her.

Her question caught Skyler off guard. Unsure how best to answer her, he told her what little he could. "I'm on my way to take care of a legal matter. Since I started out late, I was trying to make up time by traveling the last few miles to Boonville before stopping for the night."

"Where do you live?"

He looked over at her, wondering if she had any idea who he was and that he was here because of her sister. "I've been living in St. Louis for the last three years with my cousins. After I'm done with the business that brought me here, I'm going to Fayette to open my own law practice."

She recognized the town as the one Sam and her family was going to and wished this man could take her with him. "How did you choose that town?"

"My aunt and uncle that raised me live there, as well as my cousin who named my horse." He had to get her attention off him, as he didn't want her asking a question he would have to lie to. "Are you going to miss your life in Charlottesville?"

Thinking about marrying a man she didn't know, one old enough to be her grandfather made her miss her home all that much more. "Yes, but I don't have a choice in the matter," she said, but didn't explain.

"I'm sorry."

"Me too."

Then they were quiet, each busy wishing they could have a future with the other, without knowing that the other felt the same way.

CHAPTER SEVEN
Samantha & Cassidy

While Brock was in town searching for his daughter, Samantha and Andrea were saying goodbye to each other, wishing they didn't have to part.

Samantha gave Andrea a hug. "I'm going to miss you. I hope things go well for you and the baby."

"I wish I was going with you," Andrea cried, holding tightly to Samantha.

"I wish you were too," she said. Slowly she moved back from her friend and handed her a piece of paper. "I wrote down the Stoltes' address for you. If you should need me for any reason, you know where to find me."

"I hate my husband so much that I wish he would drop dead. If he did, then I could go to Fayette with you and your family."

Samantha was saddened by her friend's heartbreaking confession. "Andrea, I'll pray a rattler will get him, then you'll be free to do whatever you want."

"Then I could find a good man. A nice and loving husband, someone who isn't old enough to be my father," Andrea muttered, fighting back her tears. "I want someone like the man you're getting."

Samantha hugged her again. "I wish you had that too. Promise you'll write. I want to know all about the baby," she said.

"I promise I will. I better get back to the wagon before Boone comes looking for me."

"Good luck with the rest of your trip."

"Thanks." She waved good-bye as she hurried towards her wagon.

Worrying about Andrea, Samantha jumped when someone's hand touched her arm.

"I didn't mean to startle you," Cassidy said to her.

Samantha looked at the man she was going to marry. "I wish I could do something for her."

"I know, but she's married to Boone, so there isn't anything you can do. Your brothers want to get to Fayette today, so we need to get going, otherwise we won't have time to stop in town to get married."

Samantha blushed at his comment. "I'm ready," she replied.

She went to her wagon and climbed up, once she was seated, she looked back at Andrea's wagon one last time, then flip the reins and started her wagon to follow the Stoltes. Cassidy rode his horse beside her wagon, while Drew and Corey brought up the rear in the last wagon.

When they stopped in Boonville, Cassidy helped Samantha down from her wagon and they walked to the mercantile together. Samantha bought three dresses, planning to use the more colorful one of them as her wedding dress. After she paid for purchases, she and Cassidy return to her wagon, where she hurried inside and quickly changed into the dress.

When she stepped outside, Cassidy let out a soft whistle of admiration and her brothers complemented how beautiful she looked. She wished she still had her beautiful long hair, as maybe, just maybe she would have felt that she had deserve the whistle and complements. As the four of them walked to the church, she wished her parents were here to see her get married, but it wasn't meant to be.

When they found out the minister was out town and wouldn't be back until late the next afternoon, Samantha busted into tears, as she knew her brothers wouldn't want to wait in town all day for the minister to return. Soon she was in Cassidy's strong arms as he embraced her, trying to comfort her.

"Don't cry Sam. Drew and I don't mind staying an extra day in town," Corey told his sister, as he patted her back.

"I know how much you wanted to get to Fayette today. I suppose Fayette will have a minister there but what if it doesn't. I so wanted to be married today," she whispered. When she realized what she had just said, she looked up at Cassidy and blushed. When she saw his sappy grin covering his face, her blushed deepened.

"You and I could stay in town and your brothers could go on. We could get married tomorrow and then join them."

"Excuse me," said a man, who had walked up to them without any of them noticing him approaching their group.

"Yes," Cassidy said to the man.

"I happened to overhear your dilemma. I'm Judge William Walker, I can officiate your wedding for you."

"You can?" Cassidy asked and the man nodded. "That would be wonderful. When can you do it?"

"If you'll follow me over to my office, I can do it now."

"That would be great," Cassidy told the judge.

"Let me run over to get the Stoltes," Drew told his sister. "We'll meet you there."

She nodded, then she and Cassidy followed the man towards his office.

"Samantha, wait," a woman's voice called out to them.

She turned at the sound of the familiar voice, and was surprised to see Gwen hurrying towards her.

"Samantha, what are you doing here? I thought you and your family would be on your way to Fayette by now."

"We stopped here in town so Cassidy and I could be married."

Gwen screamed a happy shriek, as she was unaware of Cassidy's proposal. "That's wonderful." She grabbed hold of her friend. "You won't guess what has happened to me since we last saw each other."

"What?" Samantha asked, thinking it couldn't be too exciting with Felix as her husband, so she wasn't at all prepared for her friend's answer.

"Felix's dead."

"Oh, no!" Samantha grabbed hold of Gwen's hand. "What are you going to do now?"

"A handsome young man has asked me to marry him, and after the wedding, we're going to Fayette. Hopefully, we'll live at my grandfather's place."

Samantha tried to hide her shock at her announcement. "Do you know anything about this man?"

"Not really, but he's going to take care of me and the baby." Gwen didn't tell Samantha, Tucker was the reason her husband was dead, as how could she explain marrying the man that had killed her husband.

"I hope it goes well for you."

"There he is now. Tucker," she called and waved to get his attention. When Tucker reached them, Gwen quickly made introduction to the Samantha and Cassidy.

Samantha was pleasantly surprised to see the man who was going to marry Gwen, as he didn't look like the kind of man to get drunk and beat his wife, nor was he all that much older than Gwen was. She was happy her friend had found a good man to take care of her and the baby.

After Cassidy introduced the judge to the other couple, Tucker suggested to Gwen that they get married after the judge completed Samantha and Cassidy's ceremony.

When Drew and the Stolte family arrived at the judge's office there were more introductions between the newcomers, then the service was quickly performed for the two couples. Congratulations were said and then everyone returned to their wagons so they could finish their journey.

With the Stoltes' wagon leading the way, their little caravan moved out towards the next town. The Tyson brothers' wagon came next, with Samantha and her new husband following her brothers, and Gwen's wagon, which had Tucker's horse tied to the back, brought up the rear.

CHAPTER EIGHT
Andrea and Blake

As Jethro's wagon train started out that morning, it had five less wagons than it had when they'd arrived in Boonville yesterday. Four of the five wagons were on their way to Fayette, while Brock Collagen's wagon sat all alone in the field.

The group had only traveled for two hours when a wheel of the Vorbeck's wagon broke, throwing Ruth and Earl to the ground as it crashed to one side. They weren't seriously injured, but Ruth was quite shaking up.

While the other men worked to replace the broken wheel, Boone decided to rest against his wagon wheel to watch the others work. Unbeknown to him, he happened to park his wagon on top of a nest of poisonous snakes, thus upsetting the sleeping rattlers. So, when he sat down on the ground, several of the angry reptiles crept out and attacked him.

Andrea had stepped away into the forest to have private moment to relive her full bladder, but when she heard someone scream, she hurried back towards the wagons the best she could in her delicate condition. When she got closer, the group moved away to let her through and it was then that she saw her husband lying on the ground with Jethro beside him.

It was at that exact moment, she felt the first contraction surge through her belly, but with her eyes on the scene in front of her, she knew worrying about childbirth had to come later.

"What happened?" she asked Jethro.

"Several timber rattlesnakes bit him," Earl Vorbeck told her quietly.

She watched in horror as Jethro took his knife and cut into Boone leg. As her husband thrashed around in pain, Jethro quickly bent down to put his lips on her husband's leg.

"What's he doing?" she asked out loud, confused to what was happening.

"He's trying to get some of the venom out," someone responded.

"Oh!" Andrea couldn't believe this. Samantha had said she was going pray for this to happen to him, but she seriously doubted that's why he'd been attacked. "Is he going to live?" she asked. She tried not to show her excitement at the possibility of him dying, as she couldn't let the others know her true feelings of the possibility of her husband's pending death.

When Jethro moved away from Boone, he glanced down at the bite. Seeing it was starting to swell, along with Boone thrashing around in pain, he didn't think the man would last the day. He wasn't sure how to tell Boone's pregnant wife he thought her husband was going to die, but he had to say something to prepare her for Boon's pending death.

He stood and walked to where Andrea was standing. "I'm sorry, Mrs. Farrell, I don't know how much of the poison I got out. We'll just have to wait to see what happens next, but

I must tell you it doesn't look good. We'll know in the next few minutes if he's going to survive," Jethro told her. "Men, help me get him to the wagon."

But before they could move him, Boone turned and vomited on to the ground. Jethro just shook his head, as this was a bad sign.

Earl Vorbeck and Abe Combs helped Jethro carry Boone into the wagon. When they stepped out, Jethro assisted Andrea into the wagon, before following in behind her.

"Mrs. Farrell, my guess is Boone has less than a few hours to live. Do you want me to stay with you until the end?"

She bit her lip to prevent from smiling at hearing Boon was dying, because soon she would be free from her abusive husband. She was a good person, so she would stay with her husband until he took his last breath, but then her responsibility to him would be done.

"Thank you, but that won't be necessary. I know you're a very busy man. I'll let you know when it's over."

"We'll stay here until he's gone and will head out as soon as we've buried him."

"Thank you."

When Andrea eyes fell upon Boone, she shivered, hating the thought of staying in the wagon, watching her husband die. She was relieved when a half an hour later, Boone took his last breath. She reached over to a crate and quickly pulled out an old blanket his mother gave them, and threw it over his body. She didn't feel bad, as she'd done her duty to him, and once he was buried, she wouldn't ever think of him again. She stepped outside and went to find Jethro.

As Jethro Delaney helped dig the hole, which would soon hold the body of Boone Farrell, he wondered, how he was going to tell the man's young pregnant widow she would have to leave the train. The rules were any single woman without a family member on the train weren't allowed. Since Andrea was almost at the end of her pregnancy, the people of the train had taken a vote whether or not to make an acceptation for her. The men wanted her to stay, but the three women demanded Andrea leave the train according to the rules. Promising to make the men's lives hell, the men relented, letting the women have their way.

Andrea stood there beside her husband's grave watching the men shoveled the dirt directly onto his blanket wrapped body, as they didn't have a coffin for Boone. As each shovel of dirt hit him, she felt the tension leave her body, as his death gave her the freedom to do as she wished. She wasn't sure what she wanted to do, but figured she would eventually find another man and remarry. Hopefully the next man would be a better husband than Boone had been.

After Boone's grave had been filled in, Jethro took hold of Andrea's hand. "Mrs. Farrell, I need to talk to you alone for a few minutes."

"Of course, Mr. Delaney." She stepped away from the grave, her hands on her belly as another contraction shot though her abdomen. "What is it?"

Jethro looked down at his boots, took a deep breath, and looked up into Andrea's eyes. "I'm afraid I have some more bad news for you."

"What is it?" she asked, unsure of what he had to say.

"You're going to have to leave the train."

"I understand." She was disappointed with his news, but wasn't surprised by his statement.

"Now," he muttered softly.

"What?" She had been expecting she would have to leave the train, but his answer was a complete surprise to her. She assumes they would let her stay with them at least until the next town. "Now? Where am I to go?"

"You need to return to Boonville. You know the rules. No single women are allowed on the train without a male family member with them."

"I understand the rules, but any decent human being would at least take me to the next town."

"I'm sorry. Truly I am."

"Couldn't you make an acceptation this once? My baby's coming. You want me to give birth all alone on an empty prairie?"

His eyes filled with anger. "Of course not, but it might be days before you deliver. It's best if you return to Boonville, as it's the closest city."

"I'm in labor now," she cried, rubbing her belly as another pain blast through her. When they started this trip, she assumed Boone would be with her, but now she knew she would be alone on the empty prairie when the baby came.

"So, you say," he replied coldly.

"I've haven't any reason to lie," she cried out.

"My answer is still no."

"Couldn't you take a vote? If the other people don't care, couldn't I stay with the train at least until we arrive at the next town?"

"We did take a vote. The other women want you off the train."

She began to cry. "Can someone return to Boonville with me or at least stay with me until the baby comes?"

"There isn't anyone. Mrs. Farrell, if I break a rule for you, then everyone will want me to break a rule for them."

Andrea laughed. "If those words will help you live with yourself, then go ahead and think that. If I should die, my blood will be on your hands and I'll curse you with my last dying breath. I'm going to write a letter to your supervisor and if I should get to a town alive, I'm going to report you to your superiors. If not, hopefully someone will find my letter and mail it for me. I hope you rot in hell."

Without looking at the other members of the train, Andrea turned, with her back straight; she walked back to her wagon. She climbed onto her seat and released the brake, then slapped the reins against the backs of her oxen, and slowly turned the wagon eastward, heading back the way they'd just come. She'd fought her tears earlier, but once the others were behind her, she let them fall, as she was scared of how she was going to be able to deliver a baby on her own.

Andrea drove the wagon as long as she could, but when the contractions became extremely painful, she stopped the wagon under a big oak tree and moved to the back of the wagon. Figuring it wouldn't be long now before her baby came; she removed her dress and put on her nightgown.

As the contractions increased in intensity, more frightened than she had ever been in her life, she began to cry. She didn't know much about the birthing process. So how could she deliver her child without any help? All she knew was that this baby wasn't going to wait much longer to be born. She quickly dropped to the floor as a powerful contraction exploded through her. As her womb constricted trying to expel the life nestled in her, she let out a loud high pitch scream.

For the past five years, Blake Lancaster had been working on a ranch in Springfield, Missouri, saving every dime he could with the hopes of buying a ranch of his own someday. Recently his brother, Spencer had written him about a ranch for sale near him, and he decided to buy it so he could be near Spencer and his family.

Blake anxious to get to his brother's home, he hadn't stopped at noon to eat, not even to take time to fix himself a sandwich, as he wanted to reach Boonville before dark. Since he'd been in the saddle since early this morning, he was tired and hungry. Once he reached the town, he would have a steak for supper and crash, and in the morning, he would start out for Spencer's place in Fayette.

When he saw a speck on the horizon, which looked like a covered wagon, he had to take a second look to make sure the vision before him wasn't an illusion. Why would one covered wagon be out here all by itself? He had passed a westbound wagon train about an hour back, but he hadn't talked to anyone as he rode by.

Had this wagon been abandoned days ago or had it been part of the group he passed earlier today? Why had they left it behind and if so, why was this wagon heading east instead of west?

Just as he approached it, he heard a woman scream out as if she was being tortured. Wanting to come to her aid, he kicked the horse into a gallop. He quickly reached the wagon, and the split second he stopped the horse and started to leap down, he heard a second scream. Afraid of what he might find, he jumped off the horse and pulled out his gun. As the horse stood there, he cautiously moved toward the wagon.

"Hello in the wagon. My name is Blake Lancaster. Are you alone?'"

"Yes, and my baby is coming." Her voice was filled with pain and fear.

"May I come in?"

A man's help was better than having no help at all. "Yes," she replied weakly.

Blake hurriedly climbed into the wagon, letting out a quick breath as he took in the sight before him. For lying on a pallet of blankets was the most beautiful woman he had ever seen in his entire life. So beautiful, that he had to lick his lips before he could speak.

"Blake Lancaster at your service," he said as he knelt beside her and took hold of her hand.

"I'm Andrea Farrell," she said, smiling at the attractive man before her.

"Where's your husband?"

"He died earlier today from a snake attack. The wagon train I was with buried him, then the wagon master kicked me off because of the rule that no a single woman is allowed without a male family member."

"Couldn't they make an exception for you?"

"Jethro Delaney told me they couldn't, and he kicked me off knowing I was in labor. If I should die, please tell someone it's his fault I died because he'd abandon me out here," she said, squeezing hard on his hand.

"Now don't talk that way."

"Please, you have to promise that you'll tell someone about what he'd done."

"I will at the first town we come to," he promised. And he would no matter what happened, for no man should abandon any woman for any reason out on the prairie.

"Have you ever delivered a baby before?" She hated the thought of this stranger looking at her most private area, but what else could she do; someone had to help her with the delivery. It wasn't as if a doctor or another woman would be riding by soon to help.

"I won't lie to you. I don't know anything about human babies being born, but I have delivered offspring of many animals."

"Name them," she whispered as another pain consumed her.

"Excuse me?" he asked with bewilderment, unsure what she meant.

"Name the different kinds of animals."

"Why do you want me to do that?" he asked, puzzled by her request.

"It would help to take my mind off my labor."

"Oh!" He blushed, and then quickly regained his composure. "The first animal I ever delivered was a litter of kittens when I was a young boy."

"I've always wanted a kitten," she said with longing, "but my husband didn't like cats."

"Maybe you will have one someday." He smiled down at her before continuing. "Over the years, I've had several dogs that needed a little extra help delivering their puppies. On my family's ranch, there were also pigs, cows, horses, and as well as a few goats. I've helped deliver each of their young at least one time or another."

"What were the goats for?" she asked, her eyes looking deeply into his.

"My mother liked goat milk." Suddenly her grip on his hand tightened to the point he was afraid she would cut off his circulation. He figured the time for the baby's arrival was upon them. "I know I'm a total stranger to you, but I need to move down between your legs."

"I understand." When she felt his hands lifted her gown up, she swiftly looked up at the wagon, ceiling knowing an unfamiliar person was looking between her legs.

"Oh, boy," he exclaimed.

Andrea's eyes dropped to his face. "What's wrong?"

"I can see the baby's head," he quickly told her. "With the next contraction, I need for you to push as hard as you can."

Andrea pulled her legs up to her chest and held them there with her arms. With her teeth clinched, she grunted, pushing with her last breath.

"That's it. Don't stop."

"I don't think I can push anymore," she replied weakly as she let her feet touch the floor.

"Just one more good push should do it."

"I can't," she cried.

"Andrea, I can't do this for you. Come on, you can do it."

Andrea took in a deep breath as she pulled her legs upwards once again, she started pushing with what little strength she had left. She released her legs as soon as she felt the baby pass from her body.

"It's a little girl."

"Is she okay?" she asked faintly, relieved it was over.

"She looks great," he said as he cleaned the howling baby with a towel. When he was finished cleaning her, he picked up a nearby blanket and wrapped it around the baby. Then he laid the infant in her mother's waiting arms. "Do you have a name for her?"

"My husband wanted the name Bertha, but I hate that name."

Blake smiled. "Any particular reason you detest that name so much?"

"It's my mother-in-law's name. That woman hated me from the first moment we met, so I refuse to give my child that horrible name. When I get to the next town, I'm sending her a letter about her son's death, and then I'm done with her. I'm not even going to tell her about having the baby."

Blake smiled at her. "You're a hard woman, madam."

Andrea smiled back at him. "I hate to ask you, but could you take me as far as Boonville?" She was thinking that if she could get that far, then maybe she could hire someone to take her on to Fayette. All she had to do was get to where Gwen, Samantha, and the Stoltes had gone, and then she would be okay, as she knew they would help her until she was back on her feet.

"Yes, of course I can."

"You will? It won't be taking you out of your way?"

"No, ma'am, it won't. I'm going to Fayette and will be going through Boonville anyway."

She wanted to ask him to take her with him so she could find her friends, but she didn't want to intrude on any more of his time. "I hope you aren't in a hurry, as taking me will slow you down. Do you have to be there by a certain time?"

"I'm going to my brother's homestead; he knows I'm coming, but not exactly when. It won't matter if I'm a day late in arriving," he told her. But in truth, he was in a hurry to get to Fayette, as he didn't want to miss the chance of buying the ranch next to his brother's place. "Do you know what you're going to do once you arrive in Boonville?"

Instead of speaking up to tell him she really wanted to go to Fayette with him, she shook her head as tears began running down her cheeks. "I guess I'll try to find a place to live, and when I'm able, I'll find a job. I don't want to return to Virginia, as there isn't anything left for me there."

"You don't have any family there?"

"All my family is gone now. My mother died a few years ago, and my father was killed last year. I'm in this predicament because of him," she said angrily.

"Why's that?" He wondered what her father could have done to make her so furious with him.

"My father was the one who made me marry Boone. They were old drinking buddies and he thought Boone would be a wonderful husband."

"But he wasn't?"

"He might have been thirty years ago, but he was fifty and I was only nineteen when we were married. He wasn't really abusive to me, but neither was he a loving man."

"How long were you married?"

"It was a year last month, the longest year of my life! I actually felt relieved when Boone died." Her face turned scarlet at her statement. "I know that must sound bad, but our marriage wasn't a good one."

"You don't have to explain anything to me," he said, watching her as she held her daughter. Since delivering the baby, Blake had been filled with a strange euphoria, one that made him want her and her child, in his life. "How would you feel about marrying me?" Blake asked, his eyes closely watching her face for her reaction to his question.

Surprise filled her face. Touched by his proposal, she gave him a soft smile. "Why would you want to marry me? You don't know anything about me. Besides I just gave birth to another man's child."

"Delivering your baby has made me want to take care of you and I'm . . ." He wasn't sure how he could tell her he was attracted to her, so he laughed instead, hoping to take her mind off of what he'd been about to say. "Besides, it's time I took a wife."

"Oh, my. This is so sudden." She looked away from him and looked out the back of the wagon. Did she want another husband? Not really, but how she could survive raising an infant without having money or any family to help her? She knew her new friends would help, but they didn't need her and her child to take care of, as they had their own family.

Suddenly he felt uncomfortable waiting for her to respond to his off-handed proposal, so he changed the subject. "You still haven't named the baby."

"What's your mother's name?"

Her question stunned him for a moment. "Her name was Grace Anne."

"That's a beautiful name, and I think it's perfect for this little one." She smiled down at her new daughter. "Hello Grace Anne. I'm your mother." The baby yawned and closed her eyes.

"I can see she's excited about her new name," Blake teased.

"I'm sure she'll appreciate it more when she's older, especially once she learns out what her name was supposed to be if Boone had lived."

Blake noticed she didn't call him her child's father, instead had called him Boone, and wondered if that was a good sign. He gave her a few minutes to reply to his proposal, but when she didn't say anything, he took hold of her hand so she would look at him. "Are you going to answer my question?"

Andrea was thrilled this good-looking man wanted to marry her, but knew she had to refuse his proposal. "Mr. Lancaster, I thank you for your lovely offer, but you should wait until you meet someone special. Once you get to your brother's place, you may meet someone and fall in love with her."

"I've already met her," he said softly, taking her hand into his.

Andrea looked up at him "You can't be serious."

"I am. I'm going to fix us something to eat, and when we're finished with our meal, I'll start us for Boonville. During our trip to town, you think about it and let me know your decision later."

CHAPTER NINE
Gwen and Tucker

As they traveled toward Fayette, Gwen began telling Tucker about her life and how she'd ended up married to a man old enough to be her father. She told him of her mother and stepfather, and the life the three of them had before he'd died. Telling him how she and her mother had struggled to make ends meet after her stepfather's death, and when her mother passed away, probably from of a broken heart, she was left broke and all alone.

Tucker let her cry on his shoulder as she continued her story by saying that when Felix had first proposed to her shortly after her mother's funeral, she had refused his offer. After months of toiling to keep all the bills paid, she knew she had to do something when the bank told her they were going to repossess the house. She didn't know what else to do, so she'd gone to Felix and accepted his marriage proposal. Had it not been for her financial situation, she wouldn't have married the man, as it had been awful being married to him.

"So, what's in Fayette?"

"I need to take care of some business regarding my grandfather estate," she said, leaving out the part about him leaving his property to her.

He assured her they could take care of her business, and then he would take care of his. The group made a quick stop along the trail to eat their noon meal, and then continued towards Fayette. When the wagons arrived in town, Tucker and Gwen waved goodbye to the other families, as Gerard wanted to stop in town before going to their new ranch.

"Now which way do we go?" Tucker looked at Gwen as he waited for her answer.

Gwen frowned as she realized she didn't have the directions the lawyer had given Felix, figuring the letter must still be in his pocket of the shirt he'd been wearing when he died. It was too late to be thinking about it now. "If I've remembered correctly, you need to turn left at the next road."

"Left it shall be."

The next ten minutes they traveled towards what she hoped was her grandfather's property. The closer, they came to his place, Gwen started recognizing some of the area, and became excited at knowing she was almost home.

When Tucker realized they were heading towards his family home, he became animated at knowing he wasn't far from his sister's home. He didn't even think about the possibility they were headed toward the Simpson place until they reached the road to the old man's property and Gwen told Tucker to turn down it.

He stopped the wagon and looked over at her. Could Harlan Simpson have been Gwen's grandfather? He hadn't even thought about it when she said she had her grandfather's business to take care of in Fayette. If her grandfather's name was what he was wanted it to be, then he was now the owner of the land he came here to buy.

"Tucker, what's the matter? Why do you have such a strange look on your face?"

"What was your grandfather's name?" he asked softly, almost afraid of her answer. "Please tell me."

"His name was Harlan Simpson. Why is there a problem?"

Tucker leaned over and gave her a big kiss on her lips. "You won't believe this, but his property is the reason I'm here."

Gwen looked at him with confusion. "I don't understand. How do you know about my grandfather's property?"

"My sister wrote me to tell me your grandfather had passed away."

"I still don't understand." Her eyes watched him closely. "What does my grandfather's land have to do with you?

"I've been trying to buy his place for years, but every time I asked to buy it, your grandfather told me he was leaving it to his granddaughter."

Gwen looked at him suspiciously, wondering if he knew who she was when he'd proposed. Maybe he had even murdered Felix in order to marry her. Suddenly she felt hurt at the thought he'd married her just because of the land. "Did you know who I was when you asked me to marry you?" she asked coldly. She hoped and prayed he hadn't, because if he had, it was too late for her to do anything about it now.

"Of course not," he insisted. "How could I?"

"Maybe you heard Felix taking about going to Fayette to claim Harlan Simpson's land. Maybe you even killed Felix to get your hands on it," she screeched at him. As soon as the words left her mouth, she regretted her accusation.

He wanted to touch her, but didn't dare, as he was afraid any contact would upset her even more. "First of all, I didn't speak to him nor was I close enough to have overheard anything Felix said at the bar. Secondly, it never dawned on me you could be Harlan Simpson's granddaughter. The last time I saw you; you were about twelve years old and had blondish brown hair." He reached out to touch her hair. "It's a lot darker now."

She gasped. "You knew me when I was a child?"

"My sister and I use to play with you, but we called you Gwenny back then, so I never connected Gwen Atwood to Gwenny Rodgers. I didn't even give it a thought that the two names could belong to the same person."

"Oh my! I remember playing with a boy and girl who lived on the next farm." Gwen's eyes began water as she tried to respond, but she was unable to form any words. She cleared her throat as her tears began running down her cheeks.

"Please don't cry," he uttered, taking his hand and wiping her tears away.

"You kissed me, and I decided then and there that I would marry you when I grew up, but then we moved away. Over the years, I forgot about you and your sister." She took a deep breath. "Here we are married and we own the ranch you've wanted to buy. I guess it means we'll be staying here in Fayette," she added, giving him a soft smile.

"If it's all right with you?" he asked her as his hand reached over and gave hers a quickly squeeze.

"Yes. This place was my home at one time, now it will be ours."

"I like the sound of that."

When they arrived at the house, he helped Gwen down from the wagon and they started for the house. When they reached it, Tucker opened the door, then bent down and picked her up in his arms. She let out a shriek of surprise and quickly threw her arm around his neck to keep from falling. He pushed the door open further with his shoulder and carried her into the house. Then once they were inside the house, he set her down and stepped back from her to look around at their surroundings.

"The place looks good," Tucker said as he looked back at her. When he saw the tears in Gwen's eyes, he was concerned about the cause. "Is something wrong? Is it the baby?"

She shook her head. "No, just remembering living here and all the love my grandfather had for me."

"I know we don't really know each other any longer, but maybe we can fill this house with love in his memory."

She smiled at him. "I'd like that."

Tucker took hold of her hand and together they began checking the place out. Besides needing some general cleaning, the house was in good shape. He told her to sit down and rest while he unpacked the wagon. Then he went outside and started carrying all her belongings into the house.

When the wagon was empty, except for Felix's belongings, he pulled the wagon into the barn. Once there, he began stacking Felix's possessions in a corner, throwing an old blanket over everything so if Gwen came into the barn, she wouldn't have to see any of it.

Once the wagon was empty, he unharnessed the horses and put them in the corral. When he returned to the house, he was stunned to find Gwen had already unpacked some of the boxes he'd brought in for her.

"Gwen, you're pregnant, you should let me do the unpacking," he said, gently pushing her away from the box she was working on.

She smiled at him, thinking if Boone had been here, he would have yelled at her for not having all the boxes unpacked and everything put away by now.

"I wanted to get some things unpacked."

"Everything doesn't need to be unpacked in one day," he told her as he helped her to a chair at the kitchen table. "After we're finished here, I'd like to go see my sister to let her know I've arrived."

"What has your sister been doing these last few years?"

"She married a man named Lester Owens and they lived in our family home, but a year ago he was attacked by one of their bulls and was killed."

"How horrible that must have been for her." She smiled as an idea began to form in Gwen's mind. "I know your sister is probably still grieving for Lester, but I was wondering if she's ready to move on."

Tucker gave her a startled look. "Move on?" he asked slowly, wondering where this conversation was going.

"Drew and Corey Tyson are good men, I thought maybe one of them might be interested in meeting your sister."

"You have to remember it hasn't been all that long since Krista lost her husband, that and she loved her husband very much. She may not be looking for another man."

"I understand."

"Do you know where the Tysons are living?"

"Samantha told me the Stoltes bought the Garrison's old place, but I don't remember where that is from here."

He laughed. "Would you believe your friend will be living on the property on the other side of us?"

She smiled at him. "So, you're saying your sister lives on one side of us and the Tysons will be living on the other." Tucker nodded. "We could have a party of some sort at our place, invite both our neighbors, and then let nature take its course."

"We could at that. Are you ready to go to my sister's place?"

"Would it be all right if you went without me? I just hate the thought of climbing back on that hard wagon seat again. That and I would like to freshen up before I see Krista again after all these years."

He smiled at her. "No, that's fine, but I want you to rest while I'm gone. When I tell Krista where I'll be living and about us being married, she's going to explode," he said with a laugh. "Once I settle her down, I'll be home."

"You think she'll be upset about us getting married?" she asked, biting her lip to prevent it from shaking as she waited for his response.

Tucker leaned towards her, putting his nose against hers. "She might be surprised, but she isn't going to be upset I married you. So, you're stuck with me."

Her eyes twinkled as she stared at him. "I don't mind being married to you."

"I'll be back as soon as I can, but in the meantime, I want you to rest. We don't want the baby coming too early, so no more unpacking today." He looked at her waiting for her to say she would take it easy, and when she didn't respond, he gave her a look to let her know that he meant what he said. "Well?"

"I promise I'll rest. I'll even go lay on the bed."

He kissed her cheek before leaving the house. He got onto his horse, and as soon as his butt hit the saddle, he kicked the horse into a gallop, and started towards Krista's place.

Gwen went to bed, but as she lay there thinking about all the work that needed to be done, she found she couldn't lie still. So, she got up and started unpacking and putting things away in her new home.

As Tucker rode towards his sister's place, he started wondering if he would have a wedding night tonight, as he didn't know much about having a sexual relationship with a woman who was in the family way. He knew he could ask his sister about it, but if Gwen ever found out he'd talked to his sister about their sex life, he might be in trouble with his new wife. Then again, if she was expecting a wedding night and he didn't give her one, he may be in even bigger trouble with her.

Krista stood outside on the porch, looking out over the horizon. Her mind full of her brother, as she was worried, he was in trouble, as he should have arrived here yesterday. As tears ran down her cheeks, she lowered her head and began praying he would show up soon.

Just as opened her eyes and raised her head, she was surprised to see a man on a horse galloping down the lane towards her. She was afraid to hope it was Tucker, so she kept her eyes on the rider. When the man got closer and she could make out her brother's face, she let out a scream, as Tucker had finally arrived.

As Tucker got closer and saw the relief in his sister's face, he felt bad for causing her to worry about him. As soon as he was off his horse, he rushed to his sister and grabbed her into a tight embrace.

"Tucker, where have you been? I was worried something had happened to you."

"Something has happened," he replied happily.

She moved away from him and quickly eyed him from the top of his head to down to his boots. "Have you been hurt?"

"No, I'm fine." He pulled her back into his arms. "It's sure good to see you. How are you doing?"

"Better now that you're here."

"How are you doing without Lester?"

"It's been hard, but I'm surviving. Jed and Eric are still working for me, that and our neighbors have been a great help."

"I should have come home sooner."

"All that matters is you're here now. I do have bad news to tell you."

"What is it?" he asked, afraid she was going to tell him something was wrong with her or the ranch.

"I'm sorry, but they found Harlan Simpson's granddaughter. She and her husband are on their way to claim his estate."

"Let's go inside and I'll tell you all about my trip."

Wondering why he didn't seem upset about not being able to buy the ranch he'd wanted for the last five years; she gave him a curious look. After they entered the house, they went into the kitchen and Krista started a pot of coffee.

As the coffee perked, Tucker told his sister the whole story of killing Felix Atwood and marrying his widow, the girl they knew as children. Krista started crying, happy that her brother had finally gotten the ranch he wanted and would be living close to her after so many years of living hundreds of miles away.

As they sat at the kitchen table, Tucker asked if Krista thought he could have a honeymoon with a woman who was five months pregnant. The question surprised her, she didn't know the answer, but was sure Gwen would let him know if she could or not. He packed a few of his belongings he'd left at the family house, saying he would pick up the rest of his belongings the next time he came out to the ranch. He kissed his sister good-bye, promising to bring Gwen over tomorrow if she was up to it, and then returned to his bride.

When Tucker entered the house, he was surprised at how many unpacked the boxes there were sitting by the door. He was furious at the amount of work Gwen had done in the short time he'd been gone. When he found her, he took hold of her hand, and pulled her to the kitchen table. "Sit," he ordered his voice cold and demanding.

By his tone, she knew he was upset, but she wasn't sure why. "Is something wrong?"

"I told you not to overdo. The house looks as if you've done two days' worth of work in just the hour I was gone."

His praise caused her heart to soar. "I didn't unload anything too heavy."

"You promised you were going to rest." Tucker shook his head. "I knew I should have taken you with me."

She smiled at his concern. "I did try to rest, but my mind was too fidgety to relax. I wanted the place to look like a home when you returned. Besides, I'm used to hard work."

"Well, you were successful as the place looks great."

"Tucker, I didn't do anything to harm the baby."

"I still don't like how hard you've worked since we've gotten here."

She took hold of his hands into hers. "I promise I won't do any more work today."

Her touch made it hard for him to think, and he had to swallow before he could respond to her. "Okay, I've forgiven you as long as you keep your promise. When I was at my sister's place, she told me how successful your grandfather's ranch had been doing the last few years. She has been checking the cattle since his death, making sure everything was okay until you arrived."

"That was nice of her. With her husband being gone, I hope it hasn't been too hard on her."

"She has a couple of ranch hands who came over to take care of the place."

"I want to thank her in some way."

"Your grandfather's estate has been paying her to take care of the ranch until you could arrive. Now that we're here, I'll be able to take care of it."

"I still want to thank your sister. Maybe I could bake a pie to take to her."

"You could, but not today," he said, sternly. "You're done doing anything except sitting down and resting."

By his tone, she knew he meant what he said. For supper, Tucker fixed sandwiches and a bowl of soup. After they'd eaten, they went into her grandfather's room and he made her sit down on the bed. Once she was settled, he started removing all of Harlan Simpson's clothes and packing them in some the empty boxes. When he was done, he took the boxes out to the barn. When he was finished with the old man's belongings, Tucker began moving their items into the room.

She blushed when she saw his shirts hanging next to her dresses in the wardrobe. Then before they knew it, everything had been put away in its rightful place and the room felt like it was theirs.

The rest of the evening, they spent reading in the parlor. When the clock struck nine, Gwen stood to get ready for bed while Tucker went out to check the horses. When she entered their bedroom, her eyes fell to the bed and she stopped. She was instantly filled with fear at the thought of being naked and in bed with a man, she didn't know any longer.

She knew he wasn't the same kind of man as Felix, but he was still a man and tonight was their wedding night. Just the thought being intimate with a man who was more or less a stranger caused her to feel faint. She sat down on the bed and took several deep breaths, hoping it would calm her.

Once she felt more in control of her emotions, she undressed and crawled naked into the bed, but once there, she wondered if she should have put on a gown. Thinking Tucker wouldn't want to have sex with a woman five months pregnant with another man's child, she decided to put on her grown. Just as she started out of the bed so she could grab her nightgown to cover herself, her husband stepped into the room. She froze, suddenly apprehensive about him joining her in the bed.

Tucker blew out the candle. She heard him begin undressing and she bit her lip, knowing it wouldn't be long before he would consummate their marriage. When she felt him pulling back the covers, she said a quick prayer, and then she felt his weight settle on the bed. She waited fretfully for him to grab her the same way Felix did, but he spoke instead.

"Gwen, I'm going to touch you now," he whispered in the darkness, waiting anxiously for her acceptance, but prepared for her refusal.

"Okay." She wasn't sure where he was going to touch her, but she was ready, or so she thought.

He was pleasantly surprised when his hand encountered her body and felt her bare skin beneath his hand. He moved his hand across her belly, trying to be tender with her, as he knew Felix hadn't been a gentle lover. His lips met hers as his hand moved upward to encounter her left breast, caressing it with a gentle stroke. When she didn't tell him to stop, he smiled thinking tonight was going to be good after all.

She'd been expecting a rough grab of her breast the way Felix always did, so when his hand softly touched her, she let out a gentle sigh. As he fondled her breast, she continued to wait for the pain, but instead of any kind of discomfort, there was only tenderness.

His touches and kisses brought her to the point of her begging him to end the throbbing in her core, something she hadn't ever experienced before. Then a different kind of torture started, one she didn't know existed before tonight. The intense torment soon had her moaning in euphoria, and then they became one.

CHAPTER TEN
Samantha & Cassidy

Gerard stopped in town to ask for directions to their new ranch, and the first person he stopped just happened to be the mayor of Fayette, Clyde Usher. The two men talked a few minutes, and when Clyde found out about the Stoltes' school age children, he told Gerard the town was without a teacher at the time being, but he was in the process of trying to obtain one before school started.

Gerard brought Clyde over to the wagons to introduce him to the others. Clyde shook hands with all the men, and then he turned to Samantha and asked if she wanted a teaching job. She thanked him, but declined the offer, saying she was going to be busy helping the Stoltes with their ranch.

Clyde gave Gerard the directions he needed and ten minutes after leaving Fayette, the group turned down a less traveled road. At the end of it, they saw a beautiful old house with a large red barn sitting several yards away from the house. When Esther Stolte saw the first glimpse of her new home, she let out a soft cry.

A short time later, the three wagons stopped next to the barn. Calvin and Daisy, were the first down from the wagon, and started screaming and yelling, excited to have finally arrived at their new home.

"Gerard, the house is beautiful."

"I'm glad you like it. Having four bedrooms is what sold me on it."

"That will be so nice with the baby coming," she said, her eyes tearing up.

"Honey, are you okay?"

"I can't believe this is going to be our home."

"The house is twenty years old, but I was told it was in good condition. You better wait until you see the inside before you get too excited."

Gerard helped Esther down, then they walked to the house, as the others remained beside their wagon to let them explore their home without an audience.

Samantha bit her lip as she waited for the verdict, hoping for her new friend's sake, the house would be livable. A few minutes later, Esther ran out of the house and headed straight to Samantha.

"Samantha, the house is wonderful. Come on," she cried as she grabbed her friend's hand, "you have to see this place."

Samantha left her family and went inside to see the house for herself. As she took the tour of the Stoltes' new home, she was envious, knowing her new home wouldn't be this large or as nice as this one.

"Esther, I'm happy for you," she said sincerely, smiling at her as she looked into her friend's eyes.

"Samantha, someday you'll have a lovely home too."

"I know."

Esther squeezed Samantha's hand. "Before I forget, I want to tell you what to expect tonight when you have your honeymoon."

Sam blushed at the woman's words, but didn't say anything.

"Usually, a woman's first time with a man is painful. Mine was, but it wasn't horrific. The second time we made love was still a bit uncomfortable, but I think it was more because I was still nervous."

"Thank you for telling me about tonight as my mother never had a chance to talk me about any of this. I'm scared about tonight, but I couldn't ask my brothers about it."

"Cassidy is a good man. I'm sure he'll be as gentle as he can." Esther was going to say more, but her children joined them, so she quickly changed the subject.

The men had started unpacking the Stoltes' wagon while the women been on the tour of the house. When they returned from seeing the bedrooms, they began to unpack the boxes the men had brought inside. When everything from the Stoltes' wagon was in the house, the men started unloading the other two wagons into the barn where it would be stored until the other house was built.

As Cassidy looked around the barn where the four of them were going to be sleeping tonight, he made a quick decision. He and Samantha would have to return to Fayette and rent a room at a hotel, as there wasn't any way he was going to have a wedding night with his two new brothers-in-laws bedded down just a few feet away from them. He saddled two horses before going to locate his bride, finding her in the kitchen putting away dishes.

"Samantha, I need to talk to you privately for a moment." He took hold of her hand and they stepped outside.

Looking at her new husband, she saw a peculiar expression on his face. Was there something wrong? Is so, she couldn't think what could it be? Now that they'd arrived at the ranch, was he sorry he'd married her? Panic filled her as the questions flashed through her mind.

"Cassidy is there a problem?" she asked, her eyes filling with tears.

When Cassidy saw her watery eyes, he realized he'd frightened her, and he squeezed her hand. "Yes, but it isn't anything we can't fix."

"What is it?" Was he going to tell her he wanted to end their marriage?

How does a new husband talk to his bride about their wedding night without blushing? "I can't spend on our wedding night in the barn with your brothers just on the other side of a hay bale," he stated briskly, then cringing at how bad his words sounded. "I want us to ride back to Fayette and stay in a hotel for our honeymoon."

"I'd like that, but . . .," she said, blushing, regretting she would have to tell him no. "I'm supposed to be helping Esther with the house, not running off to town with you for a honeymoon."

"Go ask her. I'm sure she'll tell you it would be okay if you were gone for a night or two."

"All right," she replied anxiously.

"Do you want me to tell your brothers where we're going?"

All Samantha could do was nod, as she found talking about their wedding night to her new husband embarrassing. She hurried to the house, her mind on talking to Esther, she didn't notice two unknown men riding towards the barn.

"Esther, is it all right if I go to town tonight?" she asked when she found Esther.

"Why are you going back to town so soon?" Esther was puzzled, worried there was trouble in paradise for the newlyweds.

"Cassidy wants to have our wedding night some place with more privacy than a hay bale in the barn. It's just for the night, two at the most."

"Take as long as you need. You have a good time and don't worry about me."

"Are you sure?"

Esther grabbed hold of Samantha's hands. "Yes, I'm sure. I was a newlywed once," she replied with a giggle. "I understand the two of you wanting some time alone without your brothers breathing down your neck. When you get back, we'll finish with the unpacking. Once we're done with that project, we'll start working on making some new clothes for the children."

Samantha kissed her friend's cheek, then ran outside to the barn so she could pack a bag to take to town with her.

Gerard, Drew, and Corey came out of the barn to join Cassidy when they heard the horses arriving in the yard. The two men stepped down from their horses, introducing themselves as Spencer Lancaster and Taylor Whittaker, two of their neighbors. When Gerard mentioned they were going to build two more houses on the property, Taylor offered the service of some the other neighbors to help get the first one started.

"Since the first house is going to be Samantha and my home, I want to pay for the lumber. I've never built a house, so I don't know what to order or how much," Cassidy told the men.

The two Tyson brothers were flabbergasted by Cassidy's offer, but since it was going to be Samantha's home, they didn't say anything to dispute his offer.

"Don't worry about any of that. Just tell us how big of a house you want, and while we're in town, we can place the order for you," Taylor Whittaker told him.

"When can you pay for the lumber?" Spencer asked Cassidy.

"I'm going to going into town later today, so I can pay for it as soon as I get there."

"That would be perfect," Spencer told him.

At Cassidy's comment about returning to town, both of Samantha's brothers glared at him, as they weren't happy that he was leaving his bride to go to town, but neither of them asked him why in front of the other men.

Plans for the new house was quickly draw up, and then Spencer and Taylor left for town to put in the building material order. They would return tomorrow with some of the other neighbors to start preparing the land for the house, and once that was done, they would pick up the material and get started building the house.

As soon as they were out of sight, the two Tyson brothers started towards Cassidy.

Cassidy watched Drew and Corey march to where he was standing, wondering why they looked upset with him. "What?" he asked. Trying not to show any fear, he faced them, ready to defend himself if need be.

"Do you want to explain why you're going to Fayette when you have a bride who's expecting a wedding night with you?" Drew demanded, thinking the worse of Cassidy.

Cassidy wanted to laugh, but was afraid the two brothers wouldn't appreciate it if he did. He took a deep breath before explaining the reason for his trip to town. "Samantha's going with me to town. I want a honeymoon with my bride without my two brothers-in-law watching over my shoulder. Besides, I don't think your sister would enjoy having her honeymoon in the barn with the animals."

"I don't like it," Drew stated, his expression showing his displeasure.

"She is now my wife."

"You better not hurt her or else you'll be sorry." Drew said, poking his finger hard into Cassidy's chest. "Corey and I'll see to it with a great deal of enjoyment."

"It's our honeymoon, so you know there's going to be pain, but I do promise it'll be the only pain she'll experience at my hands."

The two men nodded, but neither of them like the idea of Samantha being alone with Cassidy, so far from them if she should need them. They thought about going into town with the bride and groom, but before either of them could tell

Cassidy about what they planned, Samantha came running out of the house.

Cassidy turned away from his brothers-in-law as Samantha joined them. Seeing her excitement, her two brothers refrained from making a smart comment to their sister about her husband, but just barely.

"Esther said she doesn't mind if I go. Let me get some of my belongings from the barn, then I'll be ready," she said animatedly, not noticing the stressful expression on her brothers' faces.

Once she was out of hearing range, Cassidy asked the two men not to say anything to Samantha about the neighbors' offer with the house or his paying for the lumber, as he wanted it to be a surprise. The two unhappy men simply nodded.

When Samantha returned from gathering some of her clothes, she found Cassidy standing beside his horse waiting for her and she gave him a smile. She looked over at her brothers to tell them good-bye, but seeing their fierce expressions, her grin quickly disappeared, wondering if something was wrong. "Is there a problem?" she asked Cassidy, looking back at him.

Cassidy gave her a nervous grin. "They don't want us to go to town for the night."

"Why not?" Certainly, they didn't expect her to have a honeymoon with them within hearing distance from them.

Cassidy took hold of her hand. "They aren't ready to let go of their baby sister just yet."

"I'm a married woman now. It's time they learn they can't tell me what to do any longer. Do you think I should I talk to them?"

"It might make them feel better if you did."

Samantha walked to where Drew and Corey were standing. "Cassidy told me you two don't want us to spend the night in town."

Drew pulled his sister into a tight hug. "No, we don't, but we understand why you wouldn't want to have your wedding night with us sleeping just a few feet away. I guess we're afraid that if you should need us, we would be too far to help."

"Drew," she started, putting her hand on her brother's cheek, "Cassidy is my husband now. I'm confident he isn't the type of man to hurt a woman, but if I'm wrong, you have my permission to beat him up when we return," she said, giving her brother a smile.

"It would be my pleasure," Drew said, laughing ecstatically.

"Mine too," Corey added, looking over her shoulder to give Cassidy a threatening grin.

Samantha kissed both of her brothers' cheek, then she started back towards her husband.

When Cassidy heard Drew cackle, he frowned, as he didn't like the sound of it, nor did he like Corey's hostile smile he'd given him. He let out a sigh of relief when he saw Samantha finally heading back to him.

"Is everything okay?"

"Yes."

"What did Drew find so hilarious?"

Samantha simply stared at him, wondering how she could tell Cassidy about her conversation with her brothers.

"Well?" He looked at her expecting an answer that would assure him that he was going to have a wedding night.

She gave him a weak smile. "If you hurt me, they have my permission to beat you up."

"Samantha," he muttered softly, his arm moving around his new wife's waist, "you do know there's going to be pain with your first time?"

"Yes, Mrs. Stolte told me what to expect."

"Then you're saying I'm going to get trounce by your brothers when we return from our honeymoon."

She giggled. "I didn't mean that kind of hurt. I meant abuse, not something all virgins' experience their first time with their husband."

"That's good to know." He looked over at Drew and Corey, then back at her. "Are you ready to leave?"

"Yes."

Cassidy helped her onto her horse before he tied her bag to the back of the saddle, then Samantha waved at her brothers as they took off back towards town. It was a quiet ride to town, both thinking about what tonight was going to bring.

Samantha wasn't afraid of the pain she knew she was going to experience with Cassidy; her fear had more to do with removing her clothes in front of the man who she married. Would he want her to undress in front of him or would they remove their clothes in the dark? Yes, he had already seen her bare breasts, but it had been just a quick glance.

They were thinking along the same lines, as Cassidy was reminiscing about her naked breasts and could hardly wait to see the rest of her when he made her his wife in every way. He'd never been with a virgin before, so he wasn't sure how to go about making tonight less painful for her.

They arrived at the hotel, and checked in. Once their bags were in their room, they took a stroll around the town, and then ate some supper. Then before she was ready, Cassidy was closing the door to their hotel room, causing her to flinch when she heard it clicked closed.

Cassidy felt bad when he saw his bride jerk at the sound of the door closing. He went to her and pulled her into his arms, hoping to say something to soothe some of her fears, but he didn't know what it could be. So instead, he brought his lips to hers.

One minute they were standing beside the bed and the next, they were naked in it. Cassidy tried to go slow as he touched her body, afraid if he moved too fast, she would tell him to leave the bed. When he touched her breast the first time, she jerked away from his hand. He continued to kiss her, moving his lips down her neck to her right breast. This time when he touched her, she didn't move away, so he continued with his lovemaking and soon they became lovers.

Samantha looked over at her husband as Cassidy slept, smiling at knowing how hard he'd tried not to hurt her. Esther had been right about the pain, especially about the second time being less painful. The whole experience of lovemaking was so much more intense than she'd thought it was going to be. The sensations she'd felt as he touched the different parts of her body wasn't anything she had been expecting, but then, how could anyone describe sex to one who'd never experience it before.

Slowly she closed her eyes, when she opened them again, she was surprised to see it was morning. She turned her head, and found herself looking into the eyes of her husband. She gave him a nervous grin, embarrassed of all they'd done to each other last night in the darkness. She tightened the sheet to her chest, afraid for him to see her body in the daylight.

"Samantha, it will get easier. Before you know it, you won't think a thing about us being in bed naked together."

She blushed. "If you say so."

"I'll tell you what. I'll close my eyes so you can get out of bed to get dressed."

She shook her head, thinking he would peek at her once she was out of bed. "You get dressed and leave the room, and then I'll get dressed."

Cassidy laughed. "Okay, if that's what you want." He got out of bed, then wondering if she was watching him, he quickly turned, but her eyes were tightly closed. Once he was dressed, he told her he would be waiting for her in the hall, and then left the room.

CHAPTER ELEVEN
Jillian & Skyler

As they walked, Skyler kept looking for his horse, but when he didn't see any sign of him; he figured the snake must have scared the horse a great deal more than he'd originally thought. Skyler was glad when finally found Buttercup two hours later, as it meant Jillian wouldn't have to walk any further. Not only was he amazed how far his horse had traveled, he now knew why horse hadn't return to him when he'd whistled, as his reins were twisted in some tree branches.

Jillian said she was use to walking barefoot, but that was on the soft grass, not on a hard packed well-traveled road. Even with walking slowly and resting often, Jillian was still limping. He'd had offered to carry her, but she refused, as she didn't want to be any more of a bother to him.

Skyler rubbed the top of Buttercup's nose with his hand, while talking softly to him as he untangled him from the branches. Once free, the horse gave Skyler a friendly nudge with his head, causing Skyler to lose his balance and almost fall.

Jillian laughed at the horse's antics. "I guess you two are good friends."

"The best."

Skyler helped Jillian into the saddle, then mounted behind her and started them towards Boonville. A few minutes later the movement of the horse had put Jillian asleep against Skyler's chest. He wasn't surprised, for he knew she hadn't gotten much sleep last night. The warmth of her body filled his with desire, but when he tried to rearrange his body to make himself more comfortable, he just ended up moving her body even closer to his groin and had to grit his teeth as he fought to control his raging body.

When the town came to view, he let out a sigh of relief.

Instead of riding directly towards the sheriff's office to report Jillian's kidnapping, he headed to the back alley to keep Jillian lack of clothes away from prying eyes.

"Jillian, you need to wake up."

"What's wrong?" she asked, jerking awake.

"We've arrived."

When she opened her eyes and looked around, seeing that nothing looked familiar, she began to panic. "Where are we going?"

"I'm taking you to the sheriff's office."

"I would like to change into something decent before we see the sheriff."

"It's important to report the kidnapping incident as soon as possible. After we talk to the sheriff, I'll go to the hotel to tell your father you're safe and that you need some clothes."

"My family was supposed to be back with the wagon train early this morning. My father is going to be furious and blame me for missing the train. I bet he thinks I ran away again."

Again, Skyler thought. "Why would he think you ran away?"

"After my last beating, I packed a bag and ran away."

"Where did you go?"

"I went to a friend's house, but her father found me and took me back home."

"When was that?" he asked, assuming she would say she had been a child at the time.

"Last year."

Skyler choked, shocked by her comment. He didn't know anything about her father, but he did know quite a bit about her sister and none of it was good. Once they arrived at the sheriff's office, he helped her off the horse and hurried her inside.

Jack Bennett looked up from his desk when he heard the back door open, and was surprised to see the young couple entering his office. The woman was dressed in only a nightgown and a man's shirt. As he continued to look at her, he was sure he hadn't ever seen her before. The man looked familiar, but he didn't know why.

"I'm Jack Bennett. What is going on here?" he demanded, standing quickly as he reached for his gun.

"There's no need for the gun, Sheriff," Skyler said as he pushed Jillian into the nearby chair. "I'm Skyler Emery and this is Jillian Colligan, she and her family was with the wagon train that probably left town this morning."

When the young man told him his name, Jack relaxed as he recognized the man's name. Since it had been at least a couple of years since the last time he'd seen the young man standing in front of him, he hadn't realized who he was. He nodded for Skyler to continue with his story.

"Last night she was kidnapped from her hotel room here in town and taken miles away. I happened to hear her scream and arrived in time to prevent her from being raped," Skyler said, as he didn't see any reason for everyone to know the ugly truth about what had truly happened to her last night.

When she remained quiet, he figured she was okay with what he'd told the sheriff, so he continued. "This morning I tied the man to his horse and we headed back to town. We had an incident with a snake and my horse was spooked, when he reared up, we were dumped on the ground, and the kidnapper got away. We walked until we found my horse and we came straight here."

"You're saying you were kidnapped from my town?" Jack asked Jillian, trying to decide if this was the truth or some story they fabricated together.

"Yes, sir."

"Can you tell me anything about the man?"

Jillian described the man the best she could, including the noticeable burn mark on the side of his face. "For some reason the man thought I was my sister, Charissa. I told him I wasn't, and then he asked if I was, Brock's other daughter, and I'd said that I was, that's when he tried to attack me."

"How did he know your sister's name?"

"I'm not sure, but he did say something about the hotel register. Charissa had made me trade rooms with her after we checked in, so when he went to what he thought was her room, he got me instead."

"Is there anyone else in town with you besides your sister?"

"My father is here as well."

"How odd," Jack replied, his expression showed his bewilderment, wondering why her father hadn't reported her missing. "I don't understand why he hasn't report you missing yet."

"He probably assumed I ran away."

The sheriff frowned. "Why would he think that?"

"Because I ran away last year," she told him honestly. "I really need my father to know what happened. We're with the wagon train, I'm sure they're anxious to get started."

Jack frowned at her. "I'm afraid the train didn't wait for you and your family."

Jillian let out a loud sob. "My father is really going to beat me now."

"I don't see how it's your fault," Jack said to her.

"You don't know my father. Everything that has gone wrong on this trip has been my fault, and I mean everything."

"You two stay here and I'll go talk to him. I'll have your sister bring you some of your clothes."

"Could you tell her I also need shoes?"

"Sure will. I'll be right back. You two make yourself comfortable." He looked sternly at them. "I suggest neither of you leave this room."

After Jack left, Skyler knelt down next to Jillian. "You don't mind I lied to the sheriff about being raped?"

"No, I don't mind," she replied, looking down at her hands.

"Considering what you've told me about your father, I thought it would be best."

"I truly doubt the man I'm supposed to marry in Kansas City will care if I'm not a virgin or not."

Panic filled him. "You're getting married?" He didn't want to lose her to another man now he'd found the woman he wanted to marry.

Tears welted up in her eyes. "My father selling me because Charissa thinks I may steal her one of her suitors."

"I'll marry you," he said swiftly, not taking a second to think about it.

She looked up and smiled at him. "I would like that, but I doubt if my father will allow that to happen."

"Why not?"

"He's selling me to an older man." She didn't want to have to explain to him about the man she was going to marry once they arrive at their destination.

He looked at her with confusion. "I don't understand. What does age have to do with it?"

She took a deep breath. "The man I'm marrying is sixty-year-old and not in good health. He's needs someone to take care of him, and I'm the lucky one who been chosen to do it. When he dies, my father plans to resale me."

"That's horrible."

"That's my father," she replied coldly.

When the door flew open, it hit the wall with a loud bang, causing Skyler to jump up and stand in front of Jillian. When he looked to see who had entered, he wasn't surprised to see an angry man and a young woman coming into the office.

The man marched to where Jillian was sitting, giving her a hateful look, as he threw clothes and shoes at her. "What's this I hear about you being kidnapped?"

"That's what happened," she replied softly. She tried not to cry, but she was scare of what her father was going to do to her.

"Do you think I'm so stupid that I'll believe that colossal of a lie? If I was you, I would just admit you ran away again and take your punishment."

Jillian was about to give him an angry retort, which would only make matters worse, when Skyler spoke.

"If your daughter was going to run away, don't you think she would have gotten dressed, maybe even put on shoes before she left her room. That horrible man would have raped her if I hadn't come by and prevented him from attacking your daughter," he said angrily, praying her father wouldn't ever know the truth about the attack.

When Skyler had stated talking, Brock had turned to look at him. "Did you touch my daughter?" he asked as soon as Skyler had stopped speaking.

Hoping to take her father mind off Skyler, Jillian spoke. "For some reason the kidnapper thought I was Charissa. When I told him I wasn't, he was just as happy to know I was your daughter."

Brock was puzzled, as he didn't have a clue why anyone would want to hurt one of his daughters. "Describe the man if you can," he ordered, still believing she was lying to him.

Jillian didn't see how describing the man would prove anything since the kidnapper was probably a stranger to him. "The man was about your age; he had a burn mark on the side of his face, and talked as if he knew you."

Brock frowned at her words, as the only man he knew who had a burn on his face was Arnie, but why would he want to kidnap and hurt his daughter. Was he out for revenge twenty years later? "Which side of his face was the burn mark?" Brock demanded, watching his daughter closely as he waited for her answer.

"It was on the left side, near his ear."

"Sounds like a man I knew from my past. He had been engaged to Charissa's mother before I married her, but I haven't seen him in years."

Jack looked at him with surprised. "Do you think this could be the same man?"

"It's possible. He took it quite hard when Beryl married me, but that was over twenty years ago. I can't believe he waited this long to retaliate. How did he know where to find me?"

"Maybe he was already in town, and when he saw you, he quickly planned his revenge," the sheriff speculated.

"That makes sense. He probably knew Charissa was Beryl's daughter, so that's why he wanted her."

"You could be right. Your daughter mentioned you were with the wagon train," Jack said, wondering how the man in front of him would react once he told him the wagon train had left without them.

"That's right. What does that have to do with our situation?" he asked angrily.

"Jethro came into town earlier this morning to tell me they were leaving as soon as he returned to camp and you'd have to wait here for the next wagon train. They're probably too far ahead by now for you to catch up with them."

"Damn." Brock looked at Jillian. "This is entirely your fault. You did this on purpose," he hollered at her, then took the back of his hand and slapped her hard across the face.

Skyler wanted to hit the man for treating his daughter this way, but Jack Bennett beat him to it by grabbing hold of Brock's hand before he could hit her again and pushing him away from Jillian.

The man was a total ass, and he sure hoped he didn't have to deal with him when the time came and he confronted Charissa on the matter he had with her.

"I don't see how it's her fault she got kidnapped. Especially since the kidnapper wanted your other daughter," Jack informed Brock.

"You can't believe anything Jillian tells you, as she's a compulsive liar. Besides, this isn't any of your business, so I suggest you stay out of it," he replied bitterly.

"This is my town and I won't have you abusing your daughter right in front of me."

Brock shook his head in annoyance at the man's interference. "You got that right; she *is* my daughter."

"That still doesn't make it right."

"My daughter is to be married when we get to Kansas City and then she won't even be my concern any longer. Do you know when the next wagon train is due?"

"Max Weber's wagon train is usually a day or two behind Jethro. He parks in the same location for the night as Jethro does, so if you're there when he arrives, he'll probably let you join up with him. Then when he and Jethro met up next, he'll square things up with Max."

"Thank you."

"Are you heading back to the camp today?"

"Yes, I think it would be best as I don't want to take the chance of missing the next train."

"Pa, if we have to wait another day or two anyway, why can't we stay at the hotel another night?" Charissa asked her father.

"If we hadn't spent in town last night, none of this would have happened in the first place," he hollered at her. "Another night is just asking for trouble."

When she saw him getting ready to deny her request, she swiftly put her hand on his arm. "Please, Pa. It's the first good night sleep I've had since we left home."

"Fine, one more night, and then we have to get back to camp. I don't want to take a chance of missing Max Weber and have to be traveling over a hundred miles without an escort. Jillian, go get dressed so we can return to the hotel."

"There a room in back you can use," Jack told her gently.

"Thank you." Jillian went to the room and quickly dressed. When she returned to the main room, she thanked Skyler Emery for rescuing her, handed back his shirt, then said goodbye to him. Her father seized hold of her arm and roughly pulled her out of the building, her tear-filled eyes remaining on Skyler until the door closed.

Brock continued to drag her until they were in front of the hotel's desk, then he requested two new rooms. Once upstairs, he had her belongings quickly moved to the new room.

"You're not to leave your room." When she didn't respond, he twisted her arm behind her. "Do you understand me?"

"Yes, Pa," she replied quickly.

"Good. I'm going to go check on the wagon. I'll have someone bring your dinner to you."

Jillian nodded at him before closing the door behind him. Once it was closed, she leaned against it and let the tears come. How was she ever going to survive her marriage if her new husband was anything like her father?

The rest of the day went by slowly for her, but she didn't leave her room other than to use the modern inside toilet, which was down the hall from her room.

After the Colligan family left his office, Jack turned to Skyler. "I feel sorry for that young lady."

"Her father is a mean bastard. Miss Colligan told me how he likes to beat her. Now that I've seen him in action, I'm sorry I brought her back to him."

"Where were you when you lost the kidnapper?"

"We were just north of town when the incident with the snake happened, I say about a half hour ride from town. The last I saw of him; he was riding towards Fayette."

"I'll send a couple of my deputies out to go look for the kidnapper. Are you staying in town?"

Since Charissa was staying another night, he decided to wait until he was better rested before confronting her. "I didn't get much sleep last night, so I think I'll stay the night before I head out of town for home," he said, instead of mentioning his real reason for staying in this man's town.

"I'll let you know if we should find him."

"Thanks."

The two men said good-bye, and after Skyler left, Jack called out for Paul Miller, his deputy, to tell him what he wanted him to do.

After Buttercup was fed and had a good rub down, Skyler sent a telegram to his cousins in St. Louis, informing them he'd found their prey and would meet with her tomorrow. Then he went to the hotel and rent a room with the hope of getting some much-needed sleep. His plan was to lie down for a few hours, just enough to make up the sleep his lost last night, but his mind was too full trying to come up with a strategy to save Jillian from her fate to be able to sleep.

When suppertime arrived, he left his room and went downstairs to the dining room. While he ate his evening meal, he continued thinking of a way to save Jillian, but other than kidnapper the girl himself, he couldn't come up with a feasible plan to save her from marrying some old man.

Thinking something would come to him once he had a good night's rest, he returned to his room. He was exhausted, as he hadn't gotten much sleep last night because a beautiful woman's backside had been stuck against his pelvis all night. He got into bed, but when he closed his eyes, he kept picturing Jillian with another man. Since that was the last thing, he wanted to think about, he put on his clothes, left his room, and walked out of the hotel, thinking a brisk walk might help relax him.

When he saw the saloon, he promptly strolled down the boardwalk towards it. When he reached it, he went inside and quickly ordered a drink. When he finished it, he ordered a second and then a third one. The whole time he sat there drinking, he thought of Jillian and the only other thing he came up with besides kidnapping her, was for him to marry her himself, but he didn't see her father allowing that to happen.

He started to order a fourth drink, but suddenly changed his mind, deciding he couldn't help Jillian if he got drunk. He returned to his room, removed his clothes, and got into bed. With Jillian still on his mind, he closed his eyes, and because of his exhaustion and the alcohol; he was instantly asleep.

When Jillian opened her door for the servant with her supper tray, she saw Skyler leave the room directly across the hall from hers and was relieved at knowing he was nearby if she should need him. She tried to eat, but her stomach was tied up in too many knots to get much food down, so she gave up and put the tray outside her door. She spent the rest of the evening reading a book, and when it was time for bed, she blew out the lantern and crawled in bed.

As she stared up at the ceiling, she tried to relax so she could go to sleep, but no matter what she did, she couldn't settle down for every noise made her think her kidnapper was returning for her. Deciding she needed Skyler, she put on her robe and slippers before opening her door and peeked out.

The hallway was quiet as she slipped out of her room and hurried to Skyler's room. She knocked, but when he didn't respond, she tried the doorknob. When it turned under her hand, she pushed the door opened and entered his moonlit room. When she saw him lying in his bed, she softly closed the door, then silently walked to the bed.

"Skyler," she called softly, but he didn't move.

Skyler was dreaming about Jillian joining him in bed, and he let out a sigh of contentment just as she put her hand on his shoulder and shook him.

"Skyler," she called a bit louder.

He moved so fast Jillian let out a squeal when he grabbed her wrist and pulled her across his body. "Skyler, it's me, Jillian," her voice filled with panic. "Please don't hurt me."

"Jillian, what in the hell are you doing in my room?"

"Skyler, I was scared. I'm afraid that man is going to come back and get me."

"You're in a different room, just remember not to open the door until you know who's out there."

"Skyler, can I stay here with you?"

"What? You can't stay here!" he harshly told her.

"Why not?" she asked innocently as tears began to form. "I feel safe with you."

He gently touched her face. "Sweetheart, if you crawled into this bed with me, I would have to make love to you."

"You want to make love to me?" she asked with bewilderment.

"Oh, yes."

"Why?"

"Because I think you're beautiful."

His words warmed her heart, as the tears fell down her cheeks. She figured she'd already lost her virginity, so what difference did it make if she had sex with this man. Besides, if she was going to be married soon, she might as well enjoy a night in Skyler's bed before she was married off to some old man, she didn't know.

"I'll stay," she said as she moved off him. She quickly kicked off her slippers, and in a flash, her robe and gown lay on the floor.

When he saw her nude body, he grabbed hold of her arm and swiftly pulled her into his bed against his nude form. He started kissing her slowly and gently, but when she returned his kisses, he quickly moved his body on top of hers to claim her as his. He was quite shocked when he reached her barrier, suddenly realizing the kidnapper hadn't succeeded in his attack, as she was still a virgin, but not for long.

"Forgive me," he said quickly just before taking her virginity.

Due to her sexual excitement, Jillian didn't seem to notice the pain. After they made love, he held her tightly against him as his breath returned to normal. He wanted to talk about what had just happened between him, but Jillian had fallen asleep and he followed soon after.

CHAPTER TWELVE

When Jillian woke early the next morning, she saw it was still dark outside. She wasn't sure of the time, but she knew she had to return to her room since she didn't want her father to find her in Skyler's room. She jumped out of bed, threw on her gown and robe, and then hurried out of Skyler's room.

She didn't once look back at him, afraid if she did, she wouldn't be able to leave him. It wasn't until she was back in her room that she realized she had forgotten her house slippers. Knowing she couldn't leave them there for someone to find and tell her father, she turned and opened her door to creep back to Skyler's room.

Charissa had also woken early, as she was at her wit's end of what to do about finding a man to marry her. She had to find someone quickly, as she didn't have much time left before her father would find out about her condition. Since she knew she wouldn't be able to go back to sleep, she might as well get up and have an early breakfast.

After she dressed, she opened her door and was just about to step out of her room when she saw a woman leaving Skyler

Emery's room. As she continued to watch, she was quite surprised to see it was Jillian leaving his room. An evil grin covered her face, as a plan quickly formed in her head, for here was the answer to her prayers.

Charissa waited until Jillian closed the door to her room, then as soon as her door clicked close, she ran for Skyler's room. She quietly opened the door and she peeked into the room. When she saw Skyler was still asleep, she hurriedly entered the room, then silently closed the door behind her.

She quickly removed her nightclothes, then pulled back the covers. When she looked down at the sheet and saw her sister's virginal blood, she smiled elatedly. She crawled into the bed, pulled the covers over her, and then scooted as close to Skyler's body as she could without waking him. When she heard the door open, her eyes went to the door, surprised to see Jillian looking at her in horror.

Jillian shocked to see her sister in Cassidy's bed, knowing what she was up to, she started towards her with her fists clamped tightly together. When she reached Charissa, she began hitting her with all the hatred she'd had stored up for as long as she could remember.

When Charissa felt the pain of the first attack, she screamed and woke Skyler, who was quite shocked to see two women fighting in his bed. In his dazed state, he was confused to why Charissa was in his bed, instead of Jillian. He tried to break the two of them apart, but being bare under the sheet, he was at a disadvantage.

The situation worsened when Brock hearing the commotion entered the room. "What the hell is going on here?" he demanded as hurried to the bed and roughly pulled Jillian away from Charissa.

"Father, this man took my virginity," Charissa cried from Skyler's bed.

"What? You're a liar because I've never slept with you." Skyler was furious, as he had a good idea of what she was planning by her statement, but he wasn't about to let this scheming woman take advantage of him.

"Really? Then how come my blood is in your sheets?"

A wicked grin covered his face. "You have to be a virgin in order to leave blood. Something we both know you haven't been for some time," Skyler sneered.

Charissa eyes shot daggers at him. "Bastard," she whispered, wondering how he knew the truth about her.

"You took my daughter virginity," Brock screamed at Skyler. "You will marry her."

"No," Jillian cried, sickened by the fact she was about to lose the man she'd fallen in love with during her rescue.

Skyler smiled. "I haven't any problem of marrying your daughter whose blood is on my sheets," he stated.

Charissa smiled a wicked smile at Jillian, making her want to hit her sister again.

Brock quickly realized he'd found the way to marry Charissa off, so he grabbed it. "Now, everyone get dress, while I go find the minister so we can have a wedding."

"Skyler, I can't wait to be your bride," Charissa cooed to him as she clutched his arm.

"Over my dead body," he said, pushing her away from him and moving to the edge of the bed.

"See here. You just said you would marry her," Brock shouted at him.

"No, I didn't. What I said was I would marry the daughter whose blood is on my sheets; I didn't mean Charissa."

Brock reacted so fast; Jillian didn't have a chance to block her father's fist. "Slut," he screamed as he hit her across the face. "You've ruined everything."

Uncaring of his nudity, Skyler jumped out of bed, and quickly grabbed hold of Brock's hand to prevent him from hitting Jillian again. "Don't touch her again or I'll make you sorry you were ever born."

Brock's eyes filled with anger. "Get some clothes on man, there is a lady present," he ordered.

Skyler was furious by Brock's comment for he knew he was referring that Charissa was a lady, but not Jillian. "This is my room. If you don't like it, you can leave."

Charissa let out a moan of desire from the bed, causing Skyler to look towards her. When he saw her looking at his bare backside, he promptly bent down and grabbed his pants.

"Since Charissa was found in your bed, you will *marry* her. I won't have Charissa having your baby out of wedlock."

Skyler laughed. "She can't be pregnant with my child for several reasons," Skyler told Brock as he pulled on his pants. "First of all, I've never had sex with that woman, but the most important one," he said giving Brook a sinister grin, "is she's at least three months with child, if not more."

"No," Charissa's denial filled the room. "Pa, don't listen to him."

"You lying," Brock boomed at Skyler in the quiet room.

"Have a doctor check her if you don't believe me," he said with confidence.

"No," Charissa screamed at her father.

Brock was torn, as he could feel something wasn't right here. Why did this man accuse Charissa of being three months pregnant? How could he know such a thing? "Mr. Emery, what makes you believe Charissa is going to have a baby?"

"I'm a lawyer from St. Louis. I've been hired by two men to find her and have her arrested for blackmail."

"What?" Brock croaked out.

"When I heard she'd left town with a wagon train heading to Kansas City, I packed a bag and took off to find her."

"He's lying, Pa. Don't believe him," she pleaded.

"Why didn't you bring any of this up at the sheriff's office?"

"I didn't think you would want all this brought up in front of the law if it wasn't necessary."

"Tell me all of it," Brock said, knowing he wasn't going to like what this man had to say about his daughter.

"I have letters with me she sent to Vincent Arndt and Walter Bishop, and in both of their letters, she claimed they were the father of her baby. She told each of them that she wanted five thousand dollars if they wanted her to keep quiet about her condition. They are prominent men from St. Louis and she knew they wouldn't want that sort of information getting back to their hometown."

"Go on." Brock said when Skyler stopped his story.

"Her biggest mistake was choosing these two men, as they're cousins. When they realized, she was trying to blackmail both of them, they decided to fight her claim, as who knows how many other men, she has pulled this swindle on? Her other mistake was these two men are *my* cousins and I'm very protective of my family."

When Brock looked at Charissa and saw her guilty expression, he knew Skyler spoke the truth. As he looked at his favorite daughter, he was filled with disgust. She most definitely was her mother's daughter that was for damn sure, for he knew Beryl had had many lovers during the course of their marriage.

"I'm sorry about everything that has happened here today. We'll leave and forget any of this has happened." Brock started for the door.

"Not so fast," Skyler said, grabbing hold of Brock's arm.

"What now?"

"There is still a wedding that needs to be performed."

"Don't you worry yourself about Charissa, I'll find her a husband."

"She wasn't who I was referring to and you damn well know it."

Brock looked over at Jillian. "Don't you worry about her situation as she's to be married as soon as we arrive in Kansas City."

When Skyler looked at Jillian, he wasn't surprised to see her fearful expression. "Jillian could be carrying my child. You either let me marry Jillian or I'll press charges against Charissa for blackmail and she'll go to jail."

"What do you call your threat if not blackmail?" Brock demanded of Skyler.

"I call it a fact," he stated loudly.

"I'm not afraid of you," Brock shouted back at him.

"Well, you should be, as I have the law on my side."

"I have a contract for Jillian to marry, and I can't go back on that."

"Have Charissa take her place, then you've taken care of two problems with just one daughter."

At the same time Jillian's fate was being determined, Paul Miller was returning to town with the dead body of Arnie Boswell on top of his horse. Paul stopped his horse in front of the sheriff's office, then haphazardly stepped down. After tying both horses' reins to the hitching post, he entered the building, then without stopping to speak to Jack, he headed straight for the liquor bottle the sheriff kept in his desk.

When Jack noticed the man pale expression, he stood and walked towards him, and when he reached him, he touched his arm. "Paul, is everything all right?"

"No, it isn't," he said, then took a long draw on the bottle.

"What's wrong?" Jack asked

"I found our kidnapper," Paul said, then shuddered.

"What happened?" he inquired, almost too afraid of what he was going to tell him.

Paul looked Jack straight into his eyes. "You know the bob cat that's being pestering the ranchers around here."

"Yes," he replied slowly, fearing where this conversation was headed.

"Well, he won't be bothering anyone anymore."

He was relieved to know the animal was dead, but he had a dreadful feeling Paul had more news to tell him. "You killed him?"

"Yes, but not before he killed the man you sent me out to find."

"So, he's dead."

"Yes."

"Did you happen to bring the body back?"

"What there was left of him, I did."

Jack frowned. "Is the body in that bad of shape?"

"Yes, but his face was intact enough for me to make a positive identification."

"The Colligan family will be glad to hear he won't be bothering them any longer."

"I found some paper work on him, he's definitely Arnie Boswell." He cringed. "Or I should say *was* Arnie Boswell."

"That's what Mr. Colligan thought it might be. I'll go over to the hotel to tell him the news."

Once at the hotel, Jack asked the clerk which room Brock Colligan was in, then he thanked the man, and headed upstairs. When he reached the landing and heard loud voices coming from one of the rooms, he hurried towards that room, concerned what the trouble could be.

As he stepped inside and saw the occupants of the crowded room, he was astonished. Jillian had been crying and had a red mark on her face, probably a gift from her father. He assumed the girls' father and Jillian had caught the young man in bed with the other sister, as Charissa was in the bed, apparently nude, and the two men look as if fists were about to start flying.

Jack wasn't sure what he had walked into, but knew he wasn't leaving until he was satisfied with the situation. "What's going on in here?" he demanded.

Brock was the first one to react to the sheriff entering the room. "It's a private matter and doesn't concern the law."

"This is still my town, so let me decide whether it concerns the law or not," he replied harshly.

Jack turned to Skyler. "Mr. Emery, may I have your side of the story first?"

Skyler quickly explained to the sheriff about taking Jillian's virginity and Charissa's scheme of sneaking into his bed and trying to get him to marry her. He wanted to mention Charissa's blackmail of his cousins, but refrained from saying anything, as he wanted to see if Brock would give Jillian freely to him.

"Mr. Colligan, it's my opinion you should allow Mr. Emery to marry Jillian and you take your other daughter with you before she gets someone killed with her lies."

"I won't allow that man to marry Jillian as I have plans for her." Brock was ecstatic Skyler hadn't mentioned anything about Charissa's blackmailing scheme to the sheriff and smiled, feeling that the other man had lie and so he held the upper hand in this situation.

"Tell the sheriff about those plans," Skyler sneered.

"Those are personal and don't pertain to the law."

Jack looked over at Brock. "Why don't you tell me anyway?"

Brock just gave Skyler a deadly look, but when he didn't reply, Skyler spoke. "He wants to sell her to some old sick man she hasn't ever met and when that husband dies, sell her to another sick man. He wants to get his hand on some cash and get her out of his life at the same time. I took her virginity and now there's a possibility she could be carrying my child. I'm willing pay him whatever the other man was going to pay him."

"I see." Jack was unsure of how to proceed, so he turned to Brock. "How much money are you getting for Miss Colligan?" he asked the girl's father.

"Two thousand dollars," Brock threw out a higher amount than he was actually getting for Jillian, thinking there wasn't any way the other man would ever be able to come up with that kind of money himself.

"I'll pay you four thousand to marry her myself," Skyler shouted at Brock.

"Oh, my," Jillian exclaimed.

"Mr. Colligan, I think you're going to have to change your plans for Jillian. Mr. Emery is offering you twice the amount you were going to receive from the other gentleman."

"No, I want the money and Jillian. He should have to marry Charissa since he slept with her and took her virginity."

"Mr. Colligan, that's a lie and we all know it. How could I take the virginity of a woman who is already pregnant?"

Jack turned to Skyler. "How do you know that?" he asked, knowing it wouldn't be something the woman wouldn't want known to just anyone.

When Brock realized his plans were about to backfired on him, he quickly decided it would be best to let Jillian go, as he didn't want the sheriff to know the truth about Charissa. "Fine, you can have Jillian. When do I get my money?"

"Just a moment Mr. Colligan," Jack said, putting his hand out, "I want to hear Mr. Emery's answer."

"What difference would that make? I said he could marry Jillian like he wanted."

Sheriff looked sternly at Brock. "I want to hear it anyway."

"Charissa had sex with two of my cousins, then told *both* of them she was expecting their child. She asked for five thousand dollars from each of them or she'd let it be known around town she was pregnant with his baby. I might be just a country boy, but I don't think it's physically possible for her to be pregnant by both of them, do you?" he asked the sheriff.

Jack looked at Charissa, then to Brock. "Mr. Colligan, considering what your oldest daughter is guilty of, I think it would be best if you just took your pregnant daughter and left town."

"Fine, but I want the money he promised for Jillian."

"I'll go to the bank as soon as it opens to get the money," Skyler said quickly, afraid her father would change his mind about allowing him to marry Jillian.

Jack shook his head. "No, that wouldn't be right considering the situation. If Mr. Colligan and his other daughter leave, will you drop your clients' blackmailing charges against her?"

"Yes, but only after she signs a statement releasing both men of any claims on the child."

Brock thinking that maybe he could still get some money out of this situation, put out his hand to interrupt the proceedings. "Just a minute, since one of those men is the father of my daughter's child, I want some sort of financial settlement."

Charissa eyes filled with tears. "Pa, let it go," she muttered, her voice filled with hopelessness of her situation.

"No," Brock shouted. "One of them must pay for what they've done."

Charissa bit her lip before replying. "Neither of them is the father of my baby," she whispered.

"What?" he hollered. "Just how many men have you slept with?" he demanded.

Jack turned to Brock. "Like I said earlier, you take your daughter and return to your wagon. Otherwise, I may be tempted to haul you off to jail and file blackmailing charges against both of you myself."

"Fine." When Jack didn't make a move to leave the room, Brock looked back at the sheriff. "Was there something else you wanted?"

"I came up here to tell you Arnie Boswell was the man who kidnapped your daughter. My deputy found him, he's dead, and so he won't be bothering any of you ever again."

"Are you sure he was the person who kidnapped Jillian?"

"Yes, he matched your daughter's description, including the burn mark on his face."

"Thank you for telling us." Brock turned, dismissing Jack from his mind. "Charissa put your clothes on as I want to be at the campsite as soon as possible. Jillian, I'll leave your trunk at the campsite." He turned and walked out of the room without looking at his youngest daughter again.

"Mr. Emery, I expect you to fulfill your promise to Mr. Colligan about marrying his daughter. So, before you leave town, I want to see your marriage certificate"

"Don't worry Sheriff, I'll do as I said I would."

"I don't care who your family is, if you don't marry this young lady, I will find you and put you in jail," Jack threatened, giving him a look, which promised he would do just that, then he left the room.

Charissa got out of bed without trying to hide her nudity. "See what you gave up for Jillian," she purred, thinking Skyler would be impressed by her body.

"I've never cared much for used goods," Skyler uttered, keeping his eyes on Jillian, refusing to look at her sister's body.

Charissa's eyes filled with fury. As she reached out to slap Skyler, he caught the movement out of the corner of his eye, and his hand grabbed hold of it before it could encounter his face.

"Someday I hope you regret marrying my sister."

"Not in this lifetime I won't," he said, smiling sweetly at her.

Charissa put on her gown before she turned to Jillian. "I hope you rot in Hell."

"I've lived there all my life with you and father," she sneered. "Now I'm going to be in heaven with a handsome man," Jillian told her sister. "Good luck with your marriage to Jacob Cobb," she said, giving her sister a bright smile.

Charissa put her hand up to slap her sister's face, but Jillian reacted faster. Grabbing her sister's wrist in a tight grip, she bent it backwards. "I don't think that would be a good idea. Now get out of here and out of my life," she said, feeling free for the first time in her life, she roughly shoved her sister away from her.

Charissa left the room without a backwards glance, slamming the door behind her. The room was quiet as the two last occupants in the room looked at each other.

Skyler smiled nervously at her. "I guess I best go find the preacher."

"You don't have to marry me," she informed him, her eyes filling with tears at the thought of not marrying this man before her.

Skyler moved to stand in front of Jillian, gently touching the red spot on her cheek. "No, I *don't* have to, but I *want* to."

She smiled weakly at him, hurt knowing that was the only reason he wanted to marry her was because she may be carrying his child. "My mother wasn't very furtive, so I doubt I could be in the family way."

He put his hand on her arm. "It's true of you could be pregnant from our night together, but that *isn't* the reason I want to marry you. I want marry you because you have brought my heart to life, and if you're pregnant, then it'll be an added bonus."

Jillian smiled at the thought of having this man's child. "I would love to have your baby."

"Does that mean if you aren't pregnant, I can try again?"

Her smile widened. "If you are my husband, you can try as often as you'd like," Jillian said, her cheeks turning red.

"You go back to your room and get dressed, when you're done, move your belongings into this room," he said, handing her his room key. "I'll run my errands and be back as soon as I can. Make sure you don't open the door to anyone, especially your father."

"I won't," she promised, giving him a weak smile.

Skyler kissed Jillian on the cheek before hurrying out of the room. He asked the hotel clerk where the church was, then left to find the minister. When he got there, he found the church was empty, so he went to the house next to it and knocked at the door. When a woman answered it, he asked if the minister was home, and she told him, her husband was out of town until later that afternoon. Skyler was disappointed by her answer, but thanked the woman and told her he would be back later.

He was extremely disappointed, as he didn't want to wait a whole day before they were married. He wanted to make love to her again, but knew it would have to wait until after they were married. Maybe Jillian should stay in her room until they were married, but then he remembered she had been scared to be alone in it. Of course, the kidnapper was dead, so he wasn't an excuse for them to stay in the same room. But what difference did it make now if they made love again before they were married? The difference was he wanted her to be his wife the next time they made love.

When Skyler returned to the hotel, he ran up the stairs like an excited child at knowing Christmas Day had arrived. He stopped just outside the door to his room, then knocked on the door.

"Who is it?"

"It's Skyler."

Glad he was back; she threw open the door. She waited for him to tell her about their wedding, but he just continued to stand there and stare at her, she felt something was wrong. "Did you find the minister?"

He stepped into the room, pushing the door closed behind him before speaking. "No," he said, his face showing his disappointment.

"No? What are we going to do now?" she cried, her eyes suddenly filling with tears.

He reached over and quickly wiped the tears away as they fell down her cheeks. "Don't cry. It's going to be okay." He pulled her into his arms. "The minister's wife said he should be back later this afternoon and for us to be there around two."

"But what are we going to do in the meantime?"

"I need to buy a wagon so we can get your trunk."

"Skyler, I'm sorry to be such a bother. We could just leave it if it's too much trouble," she said, hoping she sounded sincere. "There isn't anything important in the trunk, just my clothes," she lied, as she didn't want him to go to any more trouble because of her. Her mother's wedding dress and teapot were in that trunk and if she didn't get it back, she wouldn't have anything that had once belonged to her mother.

Something about her expression and the sound of her voice told him she wasn't telling him the whole truth about the trunk. "Don't talk that way, as I'm going to need to have a wagon anyway. Do you want to stay here and wait for me or do you want to go with me to buy the wagon?"

"I'll stay here."

He wanted to kiss her good-bye, but refrained from doing so. "Bye."

She smiled at him, as she'd seen the desire in his eyes. "Bye." After Skyler closed the door, she sat down on the bed, and began thinking about the life she was going to have with Skyler. She grinned, as for the first time since her mother's death, she felt happy.

An hour later, there was another knock on the door. "It's Skyler."

She rushed over to open the door with a smile, rushing into his arms as soon as she opened it.

"What is it?" he asked, worried that her father had stopped by. "Does this have anything to do with your father?"

She let out a soft giggle. "No, I'm just glad you're back."

His heart glowed with warmth at her comment. "I missed you too." He pulled her into his arms, quickly bringing his lips to hers. When his body started reacting to the closeness of their bodies, he forced himself to let go of her.

"I found a wagon, as well as two horses for our trip. The wagon and the horses are ready, so I came back for you so we can retrieve your trunk." When he saw her tears, he became concerned. "Have you changed your mind about marrying me?"

She shook her head. "No, why would you think that?"

"Then why the tears?"

"They're sentimental tears. My mother's wedding dress is in that trunk."

"I thought something important must have been in there for you to be so upset. Let go get the wagon so we can retrieve your chest, and start for Fayette."

CHAPTER THIRTEEN
Andrea & Blake

If Andrea did accept Blake's proposal, then she would be going to Fayette, and then she would be near her friends. "I became friends with some of the families on the wagon train. They went to Fayette, so once we get settled, could you help me find them?"

Blake smiled at her. "Of course, I will."

"If they had still been with us when Boone died, they would have made sure the wagon master didn't abandon in the middle of nowhere."

"Well then, I guess this all worked out for best as now you'll be in the same town as your new friends."

"What does your brother do for a living?"

"He started a horse ranch a couple of years ago, which he runs with Karin, his second wife, and their two children. You get some rest, and later, I'll bring you something to eat."

"Thank you." Andrea moved the baby to her side, closed her eyes and was soon sound asleep.

Blake fixed them each a sandwich, but when he brought Andrea the food, she was already asleep. He wrapped the sandwich in a cloth and put it beside her. When he stepped out of the wagon, he found his horse nearby, happily chomping on some grass. He grabbed its reins and tied them to the back of the wagon, then climbed up to the seat of the wagon, and started them towards Boonville. It was about an hour later when he heard the baby start to cry, then the young woman talking to the baby.

"I put a sandwich back there for you," he called back to her.

"I see it. Thank you."

"Do you need me to stop?"

"No, I'm fine."

When all he heard was the sound of a nursing baby, his manhood hardened. He shook his head, surprised how the simple sound affected his body. He had to keep his mind on something else, something other than marrying this woman and having sex with her. It wouldn't happen right away, as he knew she couldn't have sexual relations for at least six weeks. Boy, they were going to be the longest six weeks he'd ever lived.

Just as he saw the town come into view, he noticed a trunk sitting all alone on the side of the trail. Deciding to check it out before continuing, he stopped the wagon and climbed down. He saw a wagon sitting nearby, but he didn't think the trunk belonged to them. When he saw a man and young woman come out of the wagon, he waved, but they turned their backs to him without returning his wave.

He figured someone must have dumped it recently, as it was too nice to have been left here any length of time without someone already taking it. He opened it up and as he rummaged through it, he was startled to see a wedding dress in it. He figured the owner must have died and instead of dragging it along the rest of their trip, the family decided to get rid of the trunk, contents, and all. It was a beautiful trunk, about four feet long, two feet wide, with a large heart etched on front side.

Thinking Andrea might find a use for it, he picked it up, and carried it the back of the wagon. After setting it on the gate of the wagon, he tied it down with some rope from his saddle, as he didn't want to take a chance of it falling off.

He returned to the front of the wagon, climbed up, and started it towards town. When they arrived in town, he happened to see the church at the end of the street, so headed towards it. He stopped the oxen in front of the church, then moved to the back of the wagon to check on Andrea and the baby. When he saw they were both sleeping, he left without wake her and went into the church to find the minister.

When Blake inquired regarding having a wedding, the minister told him to come back at two fifteen this afternoon, and he could perform the ceremony for him. Blake took out his pocket watch and looked at the time, seeing they had a half hour before their wedding, he decided to let Andrea sleep a bit longer.

He walked over to a nearby bench and sat down. As he observed the town going about their business around him, he wished they didn't have to wait to get married, as he was anxious to get to Fayette to see his brother and his family. When it was time to wake Andrea, Blake returned to the wagon. When he crawled into the wagon, he found she was already awake.

"Hello," she said softly. "Are we in town?"

"Yes. We've been here about fifteen minutes. I've seen the minister and he can perform our marriage ceremony in about fifteen minutes. Are you sure you're up to this today?"

"If Boone was still alive, I would have driven the wagon the entire day by myself, then once we stopped for the evening, I would've had to unhitch the wagon, feed the oxen, fix supper, then clean it all up. Getting out of this wagon and getting married will be a piece of cake."

"Can I help you in anyway?" he asked as he knelt down beside her.

"I need to change back into my dress." She was embarrassed to ask for his help, but there wasn't anyone else to assist her

"I'll keep my eyes closed."

She had to laugh as he'd already seen the lower half of her body, so what difference did it make if he saw the top half. Between the two of them, Andrea was soon dressed and ready for her wedding. After she was dressed, she happened to see the trunk sitting at the end of the wagon, instantly recognizing it as belonging to Jillian. "What are you doing with that trunk?"

"I found it along side of the trail. When I looked inside, I saw it had someone's wedding dress in it." Blake watched as her expression changed from one of surprise, to one of sadness. "You know who it belonged to, don't you?"

"It belongs to one of the women I made friends during the trip here. It has Jillian's mother's wedding gown and teapot in it. She and her family stayed in a hotel our last night in Boonville. When it was time for us to leave yesterday morning, Jillian's family hadn't returned, so we left without them. I don't understand why it would have been left behind."

"There was one wagon nearby with an older man and a young woman, but they didn't seem friendly."

"I just wish I knew why it was left behind," she choked, her voice filled with tears. "I hope nothing bad happen to Jillian."

Blake took hold of her hand and squeezed it. "What do you want me to do with it?"

"Hello in the wagon," a male voice called out from outside the wagon.

"Let me see what they want, then we'll leave for the church." Blake left the wagon to greet whoever was calling to them. "Yes, how can I help you?"

CHAPTER FOURTEEN
Jillian & Skyler

When they reached the campsite, there wasn't any sign of her trunk. Seeing her family wagon nearby, she wondered if her father had decided not to let have her hope chest after all.

Skyler hopped down and marched over to the other wagon, a short time later he was returning with a disheartened expression.

"What's wrong?" Jillian asked as soon as he reached the wagon.

"Your father said another wagon stopped by and picked it up," he said as he climbed up to join her.

"And he just let them," she hollered, as the tears began down her cheeks. "I hope that man rots in Hell."

Skyler pulled her into his arms. "I'm so sorry."

Neither of them said a word as they drove back to town. Since there was already a wagon stopped in front of the church, Skyler stopped the wagon as near as the church as he could. He turned to look over at Jillian. "Are you ready?"

She wished she had her mother's dress to wear today, but she knew it wasn't going to happen. "Yes," she said, forcing happiness into her voice.

Skyler helped her down, took hold of her hand and they walked towards the church. Just as they started pass the other wagon, Jillian let out a sound of excitement. "Oh, my, look over there!" she exclaimed tearfully.

"Jillian, what is it?" Skyler's face went pale as he glanced at her, unsure what she'd seen.

Her hand rose up to point at the wagon sitting in front of the church. "That's my trunk on the back of that wagon."

"Are you sure?"

"I would know it anywhere as my grandfather carved it for my mother."

Skyler stopped and turned to her. "Let's go see if whoever owns the wagon will give us your trunk."

"I hope so," she said, happy tears falling down her cheeks.

They quickly walked to the wagon. "Hello in the wagon," Skyler loudly called out when they stopped at the end of it.

A man Jillian hadn't ever seen before stepped out. "Yes, how may I help you?"

"That trunk on your wagon belongs to this woman and we want it back," Skyler demanded, ready for a fight. He gave the man a stern stare to let him know he was serious, but the man completely surprised him.

The man looked over at Jillian. "You're Jillian?" he asked the young woman standing next to the forbidding looking man.

"Yes, but how do you know that?" Jillian took a step back; shocked the man knew her name.

The man didn't respond, instead he turned and said something to someone inside the wagon. When he came back out, he had Andrea Farrell holding on to him with one arm and a baby in her other.

Jillian was shocked to see her friend, as since the wagon looked the same to her as any other, she hadn't realized it belonged to anyone she knew. "You had the baby," Jillian cried out happily.

Blake helped Andrea down from the wagon before she responded. "This is Grace Anne."

"She's beautiful," Jillian said, looking down at the sleeping infant in Andrea's arms. "Andrea, what are you doing here? Where's Boone?"

"Boone's dead. Rattlers got him."

"Oh no! That's horrible."

She removed her arm from Blake and hugged Jillian. "Thanks for the prayers," she whispered in her friend's ear.

Jillian let out a loud laugh, causing the baby to fuss. Andrea put a hand underneath the baby's bottom, giving it a light pat to comfort her daughter.

"I wish I could take the credit, but I can't. I've had my own situation to deal with, so I haven't really given much thought to anyone else," she said. Since she wasn't ready to go into detail what had happened to her, she didn't explain. "Tell me how come you're here."

"After Boone was buried, that stupid wagon master kicked me off the train."

"That's horrible," Jillian cried, grabbing hold on her friend's hand.

"That wasn't the worse of it, as I was in labor at the time. I told Mr. Delaney, but he didn't believe me. Since I didn't want to be stranded in the middle of nowhere, I climbed up onto the seat and started my wagon back towards Boonville. Luckily, Blake Lancaster came by just in time to help deliver Grace," she said, then reached over and squeezed the man's hand. "Blake, this is my friend Jillian Colligan. Jillian, this is Blake Lancaster."

Jillian looked over at Skyler. "And this is Skyler Emery."

The four people shook hands, laughing as they cross their arms over one another to greet each other.

"Why aren't you on your way to Kansas City? And why was your trunk left at the campsite?"

Jillian smiled at her friend. "To make a long story short, Skyler and I are going to be married."

Andrea gave her a started look. "I thought you were going to marry a man in Kansas City."

"I was," she stopped, and seeing the man with Andrea, she realized she couldn't tell the whole story in front this stranger. "I met Skyler and things quickly changed for the better."

Andrea sensed there was more to the story, but decided it could wait until they were alone to find out about her friend's meeting with Skyler. "So, explain about your trunk."

"My father and sister left town to stay out with wagon until the next wagon train comes through. They were to leave my chest for me, but when we got out there, you must have already picked it up."

Andrea nodded. "Blake decided to take it. Are you staying here in town?"

"No, we're going to Fayette," Jillian told her.

Andrea squealed. "So are we!"

Jillian eyes widened as she stared at Andrea, surprised by her use of the word *we*. "What do you mean by *we*?"

"Blake's brother and his family live there."

"Okay, but why are you going with this man?" she asked again.

"We're going to get married too."

Shocked by her friend's statement, Jillian mouth literally dropped open. She wanted to say something about Andrea marrying a stranger, but she couldn't since she was doing the exact same thing. Of course, she wasn't about to tell her friend they had already slept together as she was afraid what her friend would think of her.

"I've shocked you," Andrea said to her.

Jillian looked at the good-looking man Andrea was going to married and saw him smiling apprehensively at her. "A little, but I can understand why you're doing it. I know Boone wasn't a loving husband to you."

"That and I didn't ever love him."

"I hate to rush you two ladies, but Jillian and I need to get to the church," Skyler interrupted.

"You'll want your wedding dress," Andrea said quickly.

Jillian's eyes began to water. "Yes. I've been very upset about not having it, as it was my mother's dream for me to wear it on my wedding day."

"If you want to step into the wagon, you could change into your dress. When you're ready, we can all head over to the church together," Andrea said to Jillian.

"I'll be just a moment." Jillian hurriedly got in the wagon. She opened her trunk, and quickly pulled out the wedding dress, not even caring how badly wrinkled it was.

She set it aside then reached back into the trunk, moving clothes around until she came to the towel wrapped item and pulled it out and quickly unwrap it. She was happily surprised to find her teapot still in one piece, and figured Charissa must have forgotten about it being in the trunk, as otherwise she would have busted her mother teapot to retaliate for all that had happened because of her. She rewrapped the teapot and placed it back into the trunk.

Once she had her mother's dress on, she realized she needed help buttoning up the back and stepped out of the wagon. "Andrea, I need help with my dress," she asked.

"Just a moment," she called back, as she looked over at Blake. "Would you hold the baby for a moment?"

"Yes, I'll be happy too." As he looked down at the infant into his arms, he realized that he was going to be this child' father. He smiled as the thought had warmed his heart.

After she handed Blake the baby, Skyler helped her into the wagon, and then she disappeared inside with Jillian.

"Jillian, are you sure about marrying this man? How do you know he won't hurt you?" Andrea asked, worried her friend was just marrying him to get away from her father and his plans he had for her.

Jillian took hold of her friend's hands. "Andrea, he saved my life twice."

"What?" Andrea was shocked by Jillian's words. How could this man have saved her life?

"First from a kidnapper and then from the fate my father had planned for me." She hurriedly told Andrea the story, everything that is except the part about sleeping with Skyler. "I trust him with my life."

"As long as you're sure marrying him is the right thing to do."

She tightened her grip on her friend's hands. "I am. Just like you know it's the right thing for you to be marrying Blake."

"I guess you're right."

Blake watched with fearful eyes as Jillian and Andrea entered the wagon, as he was worried Jillian would try to talk Andrea out of marrying him. When he felt a nudge, he looked over at Skyler.

"Jillian isn't going to tell Andrea not to marry you."

"How can you be so sure?" he asked, hoping what Skyler said was true, as he would be greatly disappointed if they didn't get married.

"Because Jillian and I haven't known each other much longer than the two of you have."

The other man's words seized Blake's interest. "Would you care to explain?"

Skyler wondered just how much to tell him about his relationship with Jillian, but seeing how worried the man was, he knew he had to tell him as much as he felt comfortable relating. "You'll probably find out our story from Andrea, so I guess I could tell you about our meeting." Skyler then gave

Blake a shorten version of the kidnapping, explaining how he'd saved Jillian, leaving out the part about her coming to his room and them making love.

"She seems happy to be marrying you."

Skyler laughed. "I truly hope you're right."

A few minutes later, both women came out of the wagon. Skyler reached up to help Andrea down, and then he reached for Jillian. When he set her down on the ground, he didn't release her as he leaned towards her ear. "You're beautiful," he told her just above a whisper. Then regretfully, he removed his hands.

"Thank you."

"Now, let's go to the church. We don't want to be late and miss our appointment."

"Are you sure you still want to do this?" Jillian asked Skyler.

"Yes, I haven't any second thoughts. Now we best head out." He took hold of her hand and they started towards the church.

Jillian smiled at him, then looked behind her to make sure Andrea and Blake was following.

Andrea smiled at her. "Don't worry about us, we're coming."

Jillian tried to prevent her tears, but as she thought of how her life had changed for the better in the last forty-eight hours, the tears came. She wasn't worried about her life now she was marrying Skyler, just excited to get on with their life together. She wasn't sure exactly where they'd be living, but knew for sure she would be happy and safe, for the first time in her young life.

When they reached the church, Jillian and Skyler entered first, with Andrea and Blake following. After their wedding, they thanked the minister and his wife and returned to Andrea's wagon so Jillian could change out of her wedding dress.

It was quickly decided the four of them would go to Fayette together, but since it was already late afternoon, and Andrea was exhausted from today's activities, they would start out early in the morning.

Andrea and Blake went upstairs to their room so she could rest and would meet the other couple later at the hotel for supper. Jillian and Skyler went to visit the sheriff to show him their wedding document, as Skyler wanted to get the matter taken care of so they would be free to leave town in the morning

When they arrived at the sheriff's office, Skyler opened the door to the jailhouse, letting Jillian precede him into the office. When Skyler saw the sheriff, he took hold of Jillian's hand and briskly moved to the man's desk.

"Sheriff Bennett, we're here to show you proof I did as I said I would." He quickly handed the document to him. "See for yourself," he grumbled loudly.

Jack sensed the man's anger by the tone of his voice and the way he'd shoved the paper at him. He understood the man's fury, but he had to be sure this man married her as he promised he would.

"I'm sorry I had to ask for proof of the marriage, but do thank you for coming in with it. It wasn't personal, but it was something I had to know for sure. If her father should ever ask me if you two were married, now I can honestly say I saw the document," he told him, hoping what he said would help relieve the hostility in the room.

"I understand," Skyler replied stiffly.

"To make up for my request, I want to offer you Mr. Boswell's horse."

Skyler's eyes lit up with a smile that brightened his face, but now felt bad for his earlier rudeness. "Mr. Bennett, I greatly appreciate your offer, thank you."

They said good-bye to the sheriff, left the jailhouse and started for the hotel with the horse trailing behind.

"Do you have any idea where we will be living?" Jillian asked Skyler.

"Well," he started slowly, unsure how she was going to take his answer. "I was planning to stay with my aunt and uncle until I found a place to live, but now I'm not sure."

"Do you think they'll be upset when they find out we're married?"

Skyler stopped, quickly turned, and grabbed hold of Jillian's upper arms. "My aunt will be thrilled you're my bride."

Jillian let out a weak laugh. "Somehow I find that hard to believe."

"My Aunt Annabelle has been after me for three years to find a bride and settle down. My Uncle Dooley kept telling her to leave me alone, as when I was ready, I would bring home the right woman for them to meet. Now that I have a bride, they will both be happy. All I have to do is find us a home."

"What happened to your parents?" she hated to ask; afraid it might bring him pain.

"My parents, Peter and Martha Emery were killed in a freak stage coach accident when I was ten. My Aunt Velma and Aunt Tabitha, my father's sisters, were both widows and had their hands full raising their own sons. Uncle Dooley and my Aunt Annabelle offered me a home, so I went to live with them and my cousin, Rachelle. They welcomed me into their home and raised me as if I were their own child."

"I'm sorry for your lossh." Tears filled her eyes at his statement. "You mentioned your other two aunts, are they still living?"

"No, Vincent and Walter's mothers were killed during a tornado three years ago. Their fathers had been gone for many years, so now they're all alone in St. Louis. My aunts' deaths were the reason I'd been living in St. Louis, as I went there to be with Vincent and Walter after the loss of their mothers."

"I'm sure you were a great comfort for them."

Skyler laughed. "I don't know about that. They were glad I was there to take care of all the legal matters pertaining to their mothers' death, as well as their matter with Charissa, but it's time for me to return home. I miss my hometown, my friends, and the more quiet way of life."

"You mentioned you wanted to open a law practice. Do you think there would be enough work for another lawyer in Fayette?"

He laughed. "Would you believe the only lawyer they had up and left town a few weeks ago? My aunt sent me a telegram telling me to come home. Do you want to get some rest before we met your friend for supper?"

"No, I'd rather take a walk." She wanted to do anything but go to their hotel room. Even though they had already made love, she was nervous about the next time they were alone together in their room.

CHAPTER FIFTEEN

Andrea and Blake

Blake carried Andrea's travel bag to their room, then told her he had an errand to run. Since the baby was asleep, Andrea decided to take a nap before supper. She laid the sleeping child in a borrowed cradle, and then got into bed and two seconds after her head hit the pillow, she was fast asleep.

While Andrea rested, Blake went in search of the telegram office to send his brother a message to tell him he would be arriving at his place tomorrow. He left out the part about Andrea and him getting married, not that Spencer would be upset, but it was just too much information for a telegram. The reason he knew Spencer wouldn't care was because his brother's present wife had been seven months pregnant with her first husband's child and Spencer had a child from his first marriage when the two of them were married.

As Blake returned to their room, he was thinking about what his future held, hoping they had done the right thing. He entered the room quietly so not to wake Andrea or the baby if they were sleeping.

He yawned, as he was exhausted, as he hadn't stopped since before daybreak this morning. He yawned again and seeing his wife sleeping, he wanted to lie down next to her.

Afraid how Andrea would feel about him being in her bed was the only thing that stopped him.

As he looked at the inviting bed, he decided he was too tired to care how she might feel when she woke up and found him in bed with her, as he was her husband. As he took off his boots and lay down on bed next to his bride, he doubted he would be able to fall asleep, but a minute later, he was asleep.

When Blake opened his eyes, he knew he had slept. He wasn't sure how long, but when his stomach growled, he figured it had to be close to suppertime. He sat up and pulled out his pocket watch to see what time it was, and when he flipped it open, he saw it was almost five. He had just put the watch away when the baby began to fuss.

The sound woke Andrea from a deep sleep, her eyes flew opened, and she looked around the room disoriented. When her eyes reached Blake who was sitting on the bed with her, she gave him a weak smile. "I guess the wedding wasn't a dream."

"Nope, you are Mrs. Blake Lancaster," he said, waiting for her to comment on him being on the bed with her.

"I like the sound of that." As she studied him, she could tell he'd been asleep, which meant he'd been sleeping next to her. She smiled at him as him being close made her feel safe, something she hadn't experience for a long time.

When she didn't comment about him being in bed with her, he relaxed. "Let me get Grace for you." He went to get the baby, gently picked her up, and hurried her to her mother.

Andrea changed the baby's diaper, and when she was done, she began unbuttoning her dress so she could nurse her hungry daughter. Not realizing she had an audience watching, she opened her dress and brought the baby to her breast. Just as the baby took hold of her nipple, Andrea looked up, and when she saw Blake was watching her, she blushed. Yes, he was her husband, but other than him delivering her baby and them sharing a kiss at the wedding, they were still strangers.

Realizing he'd embarrassed her; he turned away as the room was filled with the sounds of the infant nursing. Blake knew he should apologize for staring at her breast, but he refused to do so. He had the right to look and more as she was his wife now. A few minutes later, the room became quiet, as Grace had fallen back asleep after getting her fill.

"Let me put her back to bed."

She handed the sleeping infant to him. "Thank you."

"I telegraphed my brother to let him know I was in Boonville and would be at his place tomorrow," he said, breaking the silence in the room.

She waited for him to say more, but when he didn't, she figured he hadn't mentioned the wedding in the telegram. "Do you think your brother will be upset about you marrying me?" When he didn't respond to her, she wondered if he'd told his brother about her at all. "Aren't you going to answer my question?"

Blake had been thinking about making love to her and hadn't heard her question. When she spoke again, he turned to look at her. "I'm sorry, I was thinking about something. What did you ask me?"

"Will your brother be upset that you married me so quickly?" When Blake laughed at her question, she became angry. "What's so funny?"

He quickly sat down on the bed and took hold of her hand. "I'm sorry, I shouldn't have laughed. For you to understand, I'll have to tell you the story about his courtship with his wife."

"Was it a short one?"

"Would you believe it probably wasn't much longer than ours?"

"You're teasing me," she replied, staring into his eyes to see if he was or not.

"No, I'm not. It might have even been shorter than ours from proposal to wedding."

"Oh, my. You and your brother are impulsive."

"Well, Spencer hasn't ever been sorry he married Karin, and I'm sure I won't be sorry I married you. Now that the baby has been fed, let's go feed ourselves."

"Are you going to tell me their story?"

"I'll tell you tomorrow on the way to their place as it will help pass the time."

When they arrived downstairs, Jillian and Skyler were waiting and they hurried to join them.

Jillian looked and smiled at them. "Perfect timing."

"You've been here long?"

"Just got here ourselves."

The two couples entered the dining room, and were taken to a table away from the busy kitchen door. As they ate their meal, they became better acquainted with each other. After they finished eating, they stayed at the table visiting until the baby woke, and the two couples returned to their rooms for the rest of the evening.

After Grace had been nurse and fallen back to sleep, Andrea put her daughter to bed. When she turned towards the bed, she saw Blake's sad expression and began to worry. "Is something wrong?"

"We didn't really think this part out very well," he said while looking at the bed. It would be weeks before they could consummate their marriage, but in the meantime, they would be sleeping next to each other. How could he sleep next to her for the next six weeks and not make love to her? "Are you sure you're okay with me being in your bed?"

"Blake, we're married, and married couples usually sleep together in the same bed. It won't be any different than us taking a nap together."

He wanted to tell her she was wrong, but he decided to remain quiet. How was he supposed to tell her that he was sexually attracted to her? This afternoon he'd been exhausted, too tired to think about her being next to him in the bed. Tonight, would be different, as he was more rested, and aching for her. He wasn't sure if he could lay naked beside her without touching her in some sexual way.

When she saw him staring at her strangely, she thought maybe he was thinking she was nervous about tonight. "I'm not afraid of you."

He grinned at her. She might not be afraid of him, but he sure in the hell was afraid of how she made him feel. "I'm glad to hear that."

"If you wanted to hurt me in any way, you could have done that out there on the prairie."

He simply nodded.

"If you will turn your back, I'll get undressed so I can put on my nightgown."

The thought of her taking off all her clothes while he stood in the room with her was more than he could take. "I think I'll go downstairs for a few minutes," he said, then rushed out the door.

Andrea frowned as she watched him leave, fretting about why her new husband had dash out of the room the way he had. Did he regret marrying her? If so, did he want to end their marriage? At that thought, she began crying, as she liked being married to the strong good-looking man who made her feel safe. She was so absorbed in her thoughts; she wasn't even aware of the tears as they ran down her face.

Blake knew he'd hurt Andrea by running out of the room the way he had, but how could he explain to her that just the thought of her standing there naked behind his back was more than he could handle just now.

As he stepped out into the hallway, he bumped into someone and quickly apologized. When the man turned and faced him, he saw it was Skyler, and laughed at seeing the other bridegroom out in the hall. "What are you doing out here?"

"I'm giving Jillian some privacy so she can get ready for bed. I guess you are doing the same thing."

"Yes," he replied, his tension-filled face saying it was more than that.

"Is something wrong?" Skyler asked, concerned by the man's expression.

Blake looked at Skyler, wondering if he could tell this man what the problem was. "I can't say."

"Blake, just spit it out."

He shook his head. "It isn't anything, but a simple case of sexually frustration."

"Oh, right. A new mother can't be having a wedding night."

"I want her so bad I'm about to explode."

"You know there are other ways to take care of that problem without actually having sex with the woman."

Blake wanted to hit himself for not figuring this out on his own. "You would think a man my age would have realized that without help from someone else."

Skyler laughed. "Well, you two are strangers. She may not want to participate in whatever you're thinking about doing, but the worse thing she could say is say *no*."

Blake smiled at his new friend, as he patted him on the back. "Go join your wife and don't worry about me." Blake waved, then turned the doorknob and reentered the room.

Andrea's head jerked up when she heard the door open, and was surprised to see Blake was coming back so soon.

When Blake saw her tears, he realized he was the cause of them and felt even worse than he had seconds earlier. He rushed to her and pulled her into his arms. "Please forgive me," he said, as he stroked his hand through her hair.

"You're sorry you've married me," she sobbed against his chest.

"No, don't ever think that."

"It's true. You ran out of here so fast it looked as if someone was chasing you."

"Andrea, the best way I can explain why I did that is that I desire you, but with you just having a baby, I can't make love to you."

"Oh!" she muttered, suddenly comprehending he wanted to have sex with her.

"I don't want to hurt you, but I would love to be able touch you and for you to touch me."

She knew what he meant by his statement. She had hated touching her first husband, taking care of his sexually needs, but she wouldn't have any trouble touching her new one. She stood, then taking hold of her nightgown; she quickly pulled it over her head.

Blake's eyes practically fell out of his head as he took in her naked body. Her breasts were full of milk, as a drop of milk leaked from each nipple, telling him the baby would be wanting to eat soon. His eyes moved downwards, surprised her belly didn't show she was a new mother, probably due to the fact she was underweight and all the hard work she'd did for the past few months. He watched in a dazed as after dropping her gown on the floor, she came to him, took hold his pants, and began undoing them.

He stood there and simply let her do it, as he was so stunned by her actions as he'd never in his life had a woman undress him. Once he was naked, she pulled him down to the bed with her.

"It's our wedding night, so let's get started on it," she said.

Blake just nodded, wondering if he was going to survive the night with this beautiful woman. Luckily, he did survive the night, but just barely.

The next morning after breakfast, Andrea told Blake she wanted to notify someone about Mr. Delaney and his treatment of her. Blake wasn't sure whom she should talk to, but suggested they start with the sheriff. If he weren't the right person, he was sure the man would know whom they needed to talk to regarding the matter of the wagon master. They left the baby with Jillian, and then went to talk the sheriff.

When Andrea told Jack what the problem was, he said he would take care of the complaint for her. And he would, because he thought it was horrible what Jethro had done to the young woman, as she could have died out there giving birth alone on the prairie.

Andrea thanked him, then they returned to the hotel to retrieve Grace and their belongings, and the foursome left the hotel together. When they reached their wagon to start on their trip to Fayette, Blake helped Andrea up, then he handed her the baby. Blake flipped the reins of Andrea's wagon and the oxen started down the road.

Jillian and Skyler followed in their wagon, with Skyler's new horse trailing behind. Jillian was smiling, as she was ready to start her new life with her husband, extremely relieved she wouldn't have to see her horrible family again.

As the foursome traveled down the dusty road towards the next town, Andrea began worry. First about seeing Blake's brother and his family and their reaction to the news of their marriage, and secondly, that Blake would regret marrying her and taking on the responsibility of an unknown woman and her newborn.

When they arrived in Fayette, Blake stopped the wagon by the mercantile, as he wanted to pick up some more supplies before heading out to his brother's place. Andrea and Jillian said their good-byes, as this was where they were parting, since Skyler and Jillian weren't ready to leave town just yet.

CHAPTER SIXTEEN
Jillian & Skyler

After Blake, Andrea, and little Grace entered the building to buy supplies, Skyler took hold of Jillian's hand, and started towards the diner, as he wanted to eat before heading out to his uncle's ranch.

"Skyler Emery!" a man's voice called out as they crossed the street towards the restaurant.

Skyler turned to see Clyde Usher hurrying towards them. "Mayor Usher, it's good to see a familiar face."

"Your aunt and uncle will be glad you've made it."

Skyler shook hands with the mayor, and then turned to Jillian. "Mayor, I'd like for you to meet my wife."

"Wife! Your Aunt Annabelle didn't mention anything about you having a wife."

Skyler smiled at his friend. "That's because she doesn't know anything about Jillian yet, as we just got married yesterday."

"How wonderful!" Clyde shook hands with Jillian. "It's nice to meet you Mrs. Emery."

"Thank you, Mayor."

"Call me Clyde."

"Then you must call me Jillian."

He nodded. "I'm so glad I ran into you. I want you to know that Royce Neubrand's office is available and just waiting for you to take over his old practice. If you have time, I can show you, his place."

Clyde talked about the town on the way to the office. When they reached it, he unlocked the door, then stepped back to let Skyler and Jillian entered. Skyler looked around the room, and within just a few seconds, he knew this office would be perfect for him.

"Clyde, this is a great office."

"It's yours to use as long as you want. You can rent or buy it, either one is fine."

"Do I talk to you about the terms?"

"Yes. I don't know if you remember, but there's an apartment upstairs. It isn't very large, so I'm not sure if you'll want to live there or not."

"Aunt Annabelle probably want us to live with them, but I think being newlyweds, we might prefer living somewhere without family."

"I don't blame you." Clyde turned to Jillian. "Do you plan to work?" he asked her.

She smiled at the mayor. "We haven't talked much about that, as we had a short courtship," she said, with a slight blush.

Clyde pretended he didn't notice the blush. "By any chance are you a teacher?"

She let out a surprised gasp. "A matter of fact, I am and I have a year of experience."

"The town has an opening for a teacher this fall if you want it."

Jillian looked over at Skyler to see what he thought, and smiled when she saw him nod. "Do I have to let you know today?"

"No, but I'd appreciate if you could let me know as soon as you can. If you don't want the job, I'll have to continue looking for someone."

"Where is the school from here?"

"It's at the end of the block. We have twelve children enrolled so far, and that includes the new family that arrived in town yesterday. They have two school age children, a boy, and a girl."

"Are you talking about the Stoltes?" she asked.

"Yes? You know them?"

"I was on the same wagon train as the Stoltes family. After we're settled, I hope to visit my friends."

"Mr. Stolte's ranch is about five miles north of here."

"The last time I saw them, they thought I was going to Kansas City. I'm sure they'll be surprised to see I'm staying in Fayette."

"Let's go upstairs and see the apartment," Clyde said as he started towards the stairs.

"Jillian, while Clyde and I will talk business, why don't you look at the apartment to see if you want to live in it or not. When you're ready, we have some dinner, then leave for my aunt and uncle's place. If you want to live here, let me know what changes you might want and we'll get them taken care of while we're out at their place."

When Jillian entered the apartment, her first thoughts were that the place was the ugliest apartment she'd ever seen. Then she remembered a bachelor had lived here and he hadn't a reason to do anything with the place to make it a home. Looking at it with a different eye, she decided this place would be perfect for them and was excited to start planning on how she wanted to decorate the place.

After arranging for the apartment to be cleaned and painted, Skyler and Jillian hurried to the diner. After they ate, they started for the Emery farm, when they arrived, Skyler's family was ecstatic to see he had arrived safely. When he introduced Jillian as his wife, his family was stunned by the news, but quickly welcomed her into their home and their hearts.

As Rachelle, Skyler's cousin, sadly watched the newlyweds, her eyes began filling with tears. As she watched Jillian with Skyler, she noticed the young woman's smile was filled with love for her new husband. She was happy for her cousin, but wondered if she would ever find a man who would make her heart dance at the sight of him. God, she sure hopes it happened to her and soon, as she wasn't getting any younger.

Then she shook her head. Why would a man want an old maid, who was still living with her parents, when there were younger and prettier women in town? She hurried into the house so the others wouldn't see her tears, and once she had her composure, she rejoined them.

CHAPTER SEVENTEEN

Andrea and Blake

After Blake helped Skyler take Jillian's trunk over to their new apartment, he returned to Andrea's wagon, surprised to find her sitting up front with the baby. He smiled at her as he climbed up to join her. "Are you sure you feel like sitting up here with me?"

"I'm doing okay; besides I don't want to miss any of the scenery. Were you a rancher where you used to live?"

"Yes, I worked on a cattle ranch in Springfield for the past five years, but I missed my family, so I decide to move to Fayette to be near my brother and his family."

"Family is important."

When Andrea remained quiet, Blake became worried. "Andrea, is something wrong? Are you feeling bad?"

"What if your family doesn't like me? Or they think badly of me?"

"Why would they think badly of you?"

"Because I married a stranger the same day, I buried my husband."

Blake had to take her mind off meeting his brother and his family "I'm going to tell you about Spencer and Karin's courtship, maybe that will help you to relax about meeting them. I've already told you Karin is Spencer's second wife, what I haven't told you is Spencer's first wife; Shelia, who was three months pregnant, was killed during a bank robbery shortly before they met."

"How awful it must have been for him to lose his wife and his child," Andrea muttered.

"At the time, Spencer was the sheriff in Columbia, a town southeast of here. When he found out about the robbery, he rushed to the bank, as he knew his daughter, Mindy and his wife were in there. He was able to kill the robbers, but he was too late to prevent his wife from being shot. Just before she died, she told she wanted him to remarry and give Mindy a mother."

Andrea's arms automatically tighten around her daughter. "How old was his daughter at the time?"

"Mindy was two, way too young to understand what had happened to her mother. Spencer decided to quit his job as sheriff, and look for another line of work. He left Mindy with Shelia's parents while he searched for a safer way to make a living."

"Mindy must have missed her father, especially since she'd just lost her mother."

"She did. One of the times when he returned to visit his daughter, his mother-in-law suggested he look in Fayette, as the town was close enough that they could visit often."

"How far is it from Fayette?"

"About thirty minutes by train. Anyway, when Spencer arrived in Fayette, he found out from someone at the bank that Karin's husband had been murdered a few months earlier, was expecting a baby, and that her land was about to be foreclosed."

"That poor woman, she must have been frantic."

"Spencer thought if the widow married him, then the young woman wouldn't lose her home and Mindy would have a mother. When he arrived at her ranch to propose, there were two evil men sitting on their horses in front of her."

Andrea gasped. "What happened?"

"As my brother got closer, he recognized them as wanted men, and instantly knew they were trouble, so he was prepared to protect the young woman anyway he could."

Her hand tightened on Blake's arm. "She must have been scared to death."

He forced himself to swallow at her touch, and had to clear his throat before continuing with his story. Leaving out the part that Spencer assumed they were there to rape, maybe even kill Karin, he continued.

"As he walked to her, he talked to the men, letting them think he was Karin's husband. When he reached her, he handed Mindy to her, and then proceeded to kill the two men before their guns could finish clearing their holsters."

"He probably saved her life."

"Karin was seven months pregnant with Landon at the time, but he didn't care, he proposed to her anyway and she accepted. He took the dead men's bodies to town and arranged a wedding. When he returned to Karin's ranch, they had dinner, and then they went into town and got married."

Her eyes widened at his story telling. "Goodness! That was quick."

"Life out here in the West is different than it is back East. People out here have to work hard, as life can be a grueling, and most don't live as long as people back east."

"I guess you're right." She was quiet thinking about what he'd just told her. "So, you don't think they'll say anything about us getting married so quickly?"

"They'll be happy for us."

"What do you think we'll do when we get to your brother's ranch?"

"There's a ranch for sale next to his, which has a nice house and barn on it. The man is getting up in years and wants to get out of ranching, so I've offered to buy it all, including all his livestock. As soon as he sells his place, he's moving to Kansas to live closer to his daughter and her family."

"How much longer until we get to their place?"

"See that house over there," he said pointing to a house that had just come into view. "That's Spencer's home."

"Where's the place you plan to buy?"

Blake pointed his finger to the north. "It's just over that next ridge. So, if I buy it, Spencer will be our neighbor."

Before she was ready, Blake was stopping in front of house. He let out a loud whistle and Andrea watched as a young man, his wife, a young girl, and a little boy came running out of the house.

When Spencer heard his brother's special whistle, he hurried his family outside, relieved to know his brother had arrived safely. Once there, he was astonished to see Blake sitting on the seat of a covered wagon, but what shocked him even more was to see a young woman with a baby in her arms with him.

"Blake, you've made it." He wanted to fire questions at him, such as who was this woman and whose baby was, she holding, but he knew now wasn't the time or place to do so.

Blake climbed down from the wagon, and then helped Andrea down. "Andrea, this is my brother Spencer, his wife, Karin and their children, Mindy and Landon."

"It's nice to meet you all."

"Family, this is my wife, Andrea and our daughter, Grace."

Andrea's eyes filled with tears at Blake's lovely statement. She turned back towards him, and gave him a sweet smile.

"Wife? Daughter?" Spencer and Karin asked at the same time.

Spencer had been after his brother to marry, but he'd been hoping he would marry a woman from Fayette. Now his questions were doubling up in his mind. How long had he known this woman? Was the child she had in her arms truly his brother's child? If so, why hadn't Blake told him anything about the pending fatherhood? Or was she after his money?

"Andrea's husband died while they were on a wagon train. After they buried him, she was thrown off by the wagon master and abandoned miles from anywhere. I arrived at Andrea's wagon just in time to help deliver Grace Anne. I drove her to Boonville, we got married yesterday, and here we are."

Blake's statement answered some of Spencer's questions, but not about the money situation. Spencer was aware for the past few years Blake had been saving every dime he made towards his move to Fayette. Did this woman know Blake had several thousands of dollars in the Fayette bank, just waiting for his arrival?

Andrea was quickly engulfed in hugs from Blake's family, including little Landon. Karin took hold of her hand and pulled her inside the house with the children, while the men stayed outside to talk.

Karin had Andrea sit down at the table and started the kettle to make them some tea. "I should tell you I'm sorry about your husband's death, but I'm not since you've married Blake. Spencer has been after him for years to find a lovely woman and settle down."

Andrea laughed. "Don't you worry about it. I didn't love my first husband, nor was he a nice man."

"Why did you marry him?" she asked, surprise anyone would marry a man they didn't love, as she had loved her first husband. Karin still thought of him, but since she'd married Spencer, she didn't have the ache of his loss in her heart anymore.

"My father wanted me to marry Boone, saying he was a good man, but he wasn't."

"Blake is. You'll never have to worry about him hurting you or your daughter."

Andrea smiled. "I'm sure you're right. He sure saved the day for me when he arrived in time to deliver Grace, as I was scared, I was going to die. I was a bit nervous having a strange man delivering my baby, but he assured me he was experienced in the basics of the process."

"From what Spencer has told me, he and his brother have delivered a large assortment of animals over the years."

Andrea laughed at her statement, thinking back to Grace's delivery. "Hoping it would relax me, I asked him to name all of them while I was in labor."

Karin laughed at her statement. "You didn't."

"I did. He thought I was a bit crazy asking him such a question."

"Did it help?"

"Yes, it did. When he listed them, at least then I knew he had some sort of idea of what he was doing."

"Yes, but you did all the work."

"That's true, but it helped to have Blake with me."

"If he's anything like his brother, he'll be a great husband and father."

"I'm sure he will be.

"Spencer told me Blake wanted to buy Melvin Jacobson's place," Karin said as she smiled at her. "Mr. Jacobson lives less than a half a mile from here, we're going to be neighbors. It will be great to have more family close by."

"You have family around here?"

"All my family is gone now, but I have a lot of good friends here. Spencer's first wife's parents live in Columbia and have become part of my family."

"Do you get along with them?"

"Yes, they are great people. They have treated me as family from the very beginning of our marriage." She laughed. "I even call them Mother and Father just like Spencer does. Now that you're married to Blake, I've gained a sister and a niece."

Spencer waited until the women and the children went into the house before asking his questions. "So little brother, tell me, does this new bride of yours know how much money you have in the bank?" he inquired, as he had to be sure Andrea hadn't married Blake just for his money.

"Don't start," Blake said sharply, as he wasn't about to let his brother say anything against Andrea. "We haven't ever talked about money so she doesn't know anything about what I have in the bank."

Spencer chuckled at his brother's quick defense of his new wife. "I didn't mean anything by my question, just a teasing question from the big brother to the younger one."

Blake wasn't fooled by Spencer's immediate denial. "Yes, you did." He gave his brother a hard glare, ready to protect his wife's good name.

Spencer knew he had to smooth the waters with his brother and do it convincingly. "Now, Blake, I really didn't. You're just being defensive. You of all people know how quickly Karin and I were married, so I don't have any rights to make any comments against you getting married just as quickly."

"I'm sorry for biting your head off like that. I can't really explain what came over me, I just feel protective of Andrea. After delivering the baby, I experience some sort of euphoria, and just knew I wanted her as my wife. After her marriage to her first husband, I'm lucky she didn't kick me out the back of the wagon when I proposed."

"I know what you mean as I felt the same way when I killed those two men who were going to hurt Karin. After the shooting when I looked at her holding Mindy in her arms, I knew I'd found the woman to take Sheila's place as Mindy's mother."

"How are your previous in-laws doing?"

"The Yeargains are doing well. In fact, they were just here. Mindy and Landon had been with them for two weeks, and when they brought them home, we talked them into staying a few days to visit."

"It's nice they've stayed close to you and Mindy after you married Karin."

"Yes, that and they have adopted Landon as their grandchild and Karin as their daughter."

"They're good people and always made me feel welcome whenever I visited while Sheila was alive. Do you have time to go over Melvin Jacobson's place with me?"

"Sure, let me tell Karin we're leaving." Spencer hurried inside to tell the women where they were going. When he returned, Blake had his horse saddled for him and he had to laugh. "Are you anxious or something?"

"I wrote Mr. Jacobson I was coming, but it's taken me longer to get here than I planned. I'm afraid he might have gotten tired of waiting and sold the place to someone else."

"Don't worry. Melvin isn't going to sell his place to anyone but you."

Blake looked over at him suspiciously. "What makes you say that?"

"When you told me you were interested in the place, I went over and talked to Melvin. I told him if you weren't here by the time he wanted to leave; I'd buy the place for you."

"What did he say to that?"

"He said as long as you were here before the end of the month, he would wait so he could sell it to you."

Blake smiled. "Thanks for talking to him. I would've hated to lose the chance to buy his place since it's so close to yours."

"Come on. Let's go buy you a ranch."

The two men mounted their horses and took off towards Melvin Jacobson's ranch. Since Blake already knew everything about the ranch, all he had to do was close the deal, so he could return to Andrea.

Spencer still insisted they looked the place over carefully, double-checking to make sure all the buildings were still in good shape. When they were done, the three men rode out to check the cattle Blake would be getting with the sale of the ranch. It wasn't as large as Spencer's place, but it was big enough for Blake and his needs. He was pleased with the appearance of all the animals, as they all looked fat and sassy.

Melvin told Blake he planned to move out immediately, the house would be free for him to move in, as all he would be taking with him would be his clothes, his wagon, and his horses. When Melvin asked the two men if they would stay to help an old man pack, Blake didn't have the heart to refuse.

They packed up all his personal belongings and then put everything into his wagon. When everything he wanted was loaded, the three men rode into town with him. They stopped at the bank and Melvin Jacobson sold his ranch to Blake.

When they finished signing all the paper work pertaining to the sale, the three men shook hands. Melvin started his wagon towards Boonville, where he hoped to arrive in time to join the next westbound wagon train. The two brothers grinned at each other, knowing they were now neighbors. Then they started for Spencer's place to get Blake's new wife and move them to their new home.

Andrea hugged her new sister-in-law, telling her to come over anytime. When they arrived at Blake's new ranch and he saw how tired Andrea looked, he decided to fix dinner while she rested. Bedtime arrived early that night, as Blake knew Andrea was exhausted.

He brought the cradle in and put it in their room, and then he left, so Andrea could nurse Grace. When she was done, she laid her daughter down in it. After she had her gown on, she got in bed to wait for her husband to join her. Dog-tired, she closed her eyes and soon was sound asleep.

It was then she started dreaming.

Her dream started with their meeting, but then suddenly it changed. This time instead of delivering her daughter, Blake started rummaging through her trunk. When he found the money she'd hidden, he took it and exited the wagon, leaving her to deliver the baby by herself. She let out a scream and sat up in bed, tears running down her cheeks.

Blake had just entered the room when she let out a shriek; he hurried to her concerned she was in pain. "Andrea, what's wrong?"

She looked at him in daze, then slowly she realized she'd had a nightmare. "I dreamt you stole the money I had hidden, leaving me to deliver Grace by myself."

"You have money?"

His question made her become conscious what she'd just told him. Should she tell him the truth about the money, or keep it a secret in case she needed it later? She shook her head, as she realized Blake wasn't Boone and he had done more for her in the short time, she'd known him than Boone ever did the whole time they were married.

"I have about two thousand dollars concealed in my trunk," she told him.

"My goodness! Where did you get all that cash?" Blake was surprised by her statement.

"My father gave it to me as a wedding present."

"How come Boone didn't take it from you?" he asked, as something didn't sound right with her story.

She gave him a weak smile before she responded. "I hid it and never told him anything about it. Luckily, my father didn't mention to Boone about giving me the money."

He was touched she'd trusted him enough to tell him about it. "Why didn't you ever use any of it to get away from him?"

"I was too afraid he would come after me if I left him. Do you want me to give it to you?" she asked, knowing as her husband, he could take the money from her.

He took hold of her hand. "I am honored you trust me enough to tell me, but you keep it for you and Grace."

CHAPTER EIGHTEEN

Gwen and Tucker

Gwen opened her eyes and looked around the room, and when her eyes fell on the man sleeping next to her, she smiled. Never in her wildest dreams, would have she thought she end up married to a man like the one in her bed. Tucker was the exact opposite of Felix, and definitely, a better lover than her first husband had been. She was still staring at her new husband when Tucker opened his eyes and looked at her, causing her to blush at getting caught staring at him.

He smiled at her. "Good morning."

She laughed. "I think it is almost noon."

"Well, it's your fault we were up all-night making love."

She giggled, as a blush crept up her neck. She let out a squeal when he reached for her and pulled her against him.

"I hope I didn't hurt the baby."

She shook her head. "The baby is fine."

"Do you think it would be okay if I made love to you right now?" His eyes bore into hers, waiting impatiently for her response.

With the sun shining into the room, she didn't want him to see her nude body. "Maybe we should wait until tonight," she said, not knowing how else to tell him she didn't want him to see her nude body.

A concern look filled his face. "Is the baby giving you some trouble?"

She felt torn. Should she just let him think last night had been too much for her or should she tell him the real reason she didn't want to make love now. She quickly made a decision based on the fact she couldn't lie to him. "No, that isn't why I want to wait."

"Then what is it?" he asked, his eyes watching her like an eagle eyeing his prey.

"Tucker, I'm five months pregnant."

"I know, you told me." He still didn't understand what she was saying.

"I don't want you to see my body," she told him, blushing slightly.

He moved his hand under the covers and put his hand on her bare growing appendage. "Gwen, I've already seen your body and I think you're beautiful."

"You have?" Panic filled her eyes. "When?" she asked, knowing he must have looked while she had been asleep.

"We're married now." He reached over and kissed her. "I haven't ever seen a naked pregnant woman, so while you were asleep, I took in my fill of you."

A look of panic covered her face at the thought of him looking at her while she'd been asleep. "Why did you do that?" she asked, as tears filled her eyes with embarrassment.

He felt bad when he realized he'd offended her. "I'm sorry if I've done something to upset you. I haven't ever been married before, so I don't know what is or isn't appropriate regarding seeing one's spouse when they don't have on their clothes."

"Tucker, you haven't done anything wrong. It's just we're strangers who happen to be married."

"We haven't always been strangers."

She nodded. "Maybe so, but we are right now."

He had to change the subject of their conversation or he'd go crazy with wanting her. "Do you feel like going over to see Krista today?"

"Yes." She was relieved their topic had moved from the subject of sex and him seeing her nude body.

"While you fix something for us to eat, I'll hitch up the wagon."

"Okay." She waited for him to get out of bed, but he continued to lie there with his hand on her belly, gently stroking it. Gazing into his eyes, she knew he was waiting for her to tell him he could make love to her. She'd only said no because she was embarrassed for him to see her in the daylight. Why should she deny both of them of something as wonderful as making love just because she was shy? "Will you keep your eyes closed?" she asked seriously.

"Gwen, I told you, I've already seen you."

"I don't care!" she shouted, closing her eyes against his intense gaze. She opened her eyes and looked at him. "Tucker, I'm sorry for yelling, but this is hard for me."

Tucker moved his hand from her belly to the side of her face. "I understand. I'm sorry I've upset you, and I promise I'll keep my eyes closed." he said, then moved his lips to hers.

After he made love to his wife, he laid there holding her in his arms, trying not to kiss her again knowing where it would lead them if he did. He knew she'd enjoyed their lovemaking, but until she was more accustomed to him seeing her body in the daylight, he wasn't going to push his luck.

He leaned over and kissed her forehead. "I'll go get the wagon ready."

"Okay," she said, then quickly closed her eyes as her naked husband got out of the bed. She waited until she heard him leave the room, then she threw the covers off and quickly dressed.

After they finished their breakfast, they started for Krista's ranch. When they arrived, Gwen was surprised how much of the place she remembered from her childhood.

"Does your sister have any kittens running around?"

"I don't know. Why do you ask?" he asked looking over at her.

"Do you think your sister may have one she wants to get rid of?"

"We can ask her."

Tucker stopped the wagon, set the brake, and then stepped down. After he helped Gwen from the wagon, and let go of his bride, she was quickly engulfed in an embrace by his sister.

"Little Gwenny Rodgers," Krista cried.

"Krista, I'm sorry about your husband."

"Thank you. Lester was a good man." Krista gave Gwen a grin, but it quickly disappeared as she looked down at Gwen's belly. When she looked back up at Gwen, she had tears in her eyes. "Lester and I tried to have a baby, but it just wasn't meant to be."

"I'm so sorry."

"I would like to remarry someday, but there isn't anyone around here who has caught my interest." She watched Gwen looked over at her husband, and then quickly back to her. No one said anything, but Krista got the impression something was going on between them. "Do you two want to explain what's going on here?"

Gwen blushed. "I'm sorry, Krista. There was a family of two brothers and a sister on the wagon train with me, and I became friends with their sister. They'll be living here in Fayette, and I thought maybe you and one of the brothers would hit it off."

Krista was touched by her new sister-in-law's idea. "That's sweet of you to think of me. Do you happen to know where they're living?"

"The man they're working for bought the Garrison's property. Once his place is up and running, they'll be building their homes on the property."

"With them living so close, I'm sure I'm bound to meet them."

"I thought maybe we could have a party and invited several families, that way they wouldn't suspect the real reason for the party was for them to meet you."

Krista laughed. "I'm sure I won't be the only single woman who'll be interested in meeting two young single men."

Gwen frowned; disappointed Krista might not have a chance with one of her friend's brothers. "Are there a lot of single women around here?"

"There are five of us, Rachelle Emery and I are both twenty-five, and Kira Wallace, Harriet Talcott, and Jayne Reid are twenty-seven, but I'm the only one who has ever been married." Krista reached over to touch Gwen's hand. "Don't worry about me. I've had my chance at marriage, I can live with the fact I may never get married again."

"Are the other women attractive?" Gwen asked, hoping she would say they weren't.

"I would say they're all more attractive than I am."

Tucker snorted and both women looked over at him. "I would agree that Rachelle is attractive, but the other three's personality takes away from any beauty they have."

"That may be true, but they are still attractive woman."

"Lester was smart enough not to fall for those three witches," Tucker said, smiling at his sister.

She simply nodded, as the memory of Lester choosing her over the other women warmed her heart. Just then, a mother cat and her two kittens stepped out of the barn.

"Tucker look, kittens," Gwen cried, pointing in their direction.

Krista laughed. "Are you looking for a cat?"

"Yes. Do you want to part with either of the kittens?"

"You can have them both if you want. They are both males, so you wouldn't have to worry about having a litter of kittens showing up at your place."

Gwen looked over at her new husband. "Can I have two?"

"I don't know, they look like they may eat us out of house and home." Tucker said, then laughed at her stunned expression. "Of course, you may have them both."

They stayed an hour visiting Krista, making plans to have the party in two weeks. Krista hugged Tucker and Gwen before they left, promising to come over in a day or so to see them.

Since they were already out and Gwen seemed to be doing okay, Tucker drove them into town so they could eat at the diner. As they stepped inside, Gwen was stocked to see Jillian and a strange man sitting there looking at menus. A lot of questions ran through her head, as last she knew, Jillian should be on her way to Kansas City to marry an older man who was sick, this man definitely wasn't old or in poor health.

She rushed to their table, and when Jillian saw her, she stood up and the two women embraced.

"What are you doing here and who is that with you?" Gwen and Jillian asked simultaneously causing the two women to laugh.

Jillian quickly explained that she and Skyler were married, they would be living in town as Skyler was taking over the previous lawyer's office and she was going to teach school in the fall.

Gwen laughed. When Jillian gave her a strange look, she explained about Felix's death and her marrying Tucker, a man she knew as a child.

She went on to tell the other couple about the party they were planning, saying how she wished Andrea had been able to come to Fayette with them. Jillian surprised her by telling her about Boone's death, the birth of Andrea's daughter and that she had married a man who did indeed live nearby.

When Tucker asked whom, she'd married, Jillian told them Andrea had married Blake Lancaster. Tucker said he knew him from when he'd visited his brother and thought he was a good man. Gwen was relieved to hear her friend was now married to a good man, and Tucker promised they would stop by to see her friend as soon as she had some rest.

After they finished visiting with Jillian and Skyler, Gwen and Tucker left Fayette, and drove on to the Stoltes' place to tell them about the party. Gwen was disappointed to learn Samantha wasn't there, but was happy to know her friend was having a honeymoon without her brothers.

Tucker expected to see some sort of attraction between her and one of the brothers, so he watched Gwen closely around the two Tyson brothers. He was greatly surprised to see there didn't seem to be any kind of magnetism by either of the Tysons towards his wife or her towards the brothers.

Once home, Tucker wanted his wife to rest after the long wagon trip, but she insisted on unpacking a few more boxes. By bedtime, she was tired, but happy with the work she'd completed that day. After they made love, she went to sleep with a kitten on either side of her leg, and a snoring husband beside her.

CHAPTER NINETEEN
Samantha & Cassidy

After Cassidy and Samantha had a late breakfast, he took his bride to the mercantile. While she was busy picking out dresses, Cassidy paid for the lumber Taylor Whittaker had ordered, telling the owner someone would be in later today to pick it up.

By the time they'd finished with their shopping, it was noon. Not in any hurry to return Samantha to her brothers, Cassidy insisted they have something to eat before heading out the ranch. After they'd eaten, he said he wanted to take her on a tour of the town.

Samantha enjoying spending the day with her new husband, hadn't realized how late it was getting until her stomach growled. When she finally realized it was suppertime, she asked when they were starting for home and Cassidy told her he wanted one more night with her before returning to her brothers.

Since she wanted the same thing, she agreed to stay in town for another night. Their second night together was mostly spent making love, and when they finally fell asleep, the sun was just beginning to make its appearance in the sky. When they woke, it was almost noon, and they laughed to see how late it was. They quickly dressed, packed their belongings, and hurried to the diner to eat before starting back to the ranch.

When they arrived at the Stoltes' place that afternoon, Samantha was surprised to see a large area had been cleared where they had talked about putting their house. As she looked around, she was further amazed to see the pile of lumber lying nearby.

She was so engrossed wondering how all this had transpired while they were gone; she just sat there on her horse, unaware of the angry man stomping her way. When a pair of strong hands grasped her tightly around her waist and pulled her off her horse, she let out a squeal. When she turned to see who had her, she was astonished to see Drew's livid expression.

"Drew, what's wrong?"

He set his sister down on her feet with more force than he meant, but didn't apologize. "We expected you yesterday," he said angrily, then looked over Cassidy, giving him an infuriated glare. "What in the hell have you two been doing all this time?" Once the words were out of his mouth, he blushed as he realized what he'd just said and instantly regretted his comment to his sister. "I'm sorry. That didn't come out right."

"Drew, aren't I entitled to have a honeymoon with my husband like any other bride?"

"Well, yes of course you are."

"That's way we're late." She took hold of her husband's hand when he joined her. "I'm married now, so I don't have to explain what I do to you. End of discussion for now and anytime in the future," she informed her brother, giving him a look that screamed she meant every word of what she'd just said.

"Are you're okay?"

"Yes, I'm fine."

Drew looked over at Cassidy, gave him an ornery grin, then turned back to his sister. "I guess that mean we don't get to pound the life out of that new husband of yours," he stated disappointedly, as he smiled at his sister.

"Not if you want to remain being my brother," she replied coolly.

Knowing someone had to break the tension that was in the air between his two siblings; Corey took his sister's hand. "Come see what we've planned for our home."

"Don't pay attention to Drew," Corey said softly as they reached the cleared space. "He's just been worried about you."

"I know." She turned to see if Cassidy was following and was greatly relieved to see he was right behind her.

"We decided it would be best if you and Cassidy stayed in the house with the Stoltes until the house's completed as it would at least give you some privacy."

"You two have been busy while we were gone."

The three men looked at each other, but no one mentioned about the neighbors who had helped prepare the land or that they would be back in the morning to help start building their home.

"Gerard said since his place was in such good shape, we could start constructing our house," Corey told her, hoping to distract her from asking how they'd accomplished so much in such a short time.

"How long do you think it will be before it's done?" She wanted it to be completed now, as she wanted to move in her new home and begin their life together as man and wife.

Cassidy laughed. "You have to be patient."

"I'm trying, but I want to start our marriage in our home."

He took hold of her hand and gave it a squeeze. "We'll be in our own home before you know it, and before long we'll have babies to fill the other bedrooms."

She looked at her husband, tearing up at his words. "That sounds so nice."

"Why don't you go inside the house to get settled in our room?"

"Okay. When I'm done, I'll see if Esther needs my help."

"I'm going to stay outside with your brothers."

She nodded, then she walked to the house to find Esther to see if she could help with the housework.

Cassidy watched Samantha until she disappeared inside. When he turned towards her brothers, he saw they had been watching him. "What?"

"You really do care for her," Drew stated.

"Of course, I do. I wouldn't have married her otherwise."

Drew shook his head. "I just don't get how you could have such strong feelings for her. You two haven't even known each other all that long."

Cassidy smiled. "I can't explain it, but ever since I first saw her, I've been drawn to her." Corey laughed at his comment, and Cassidy looked angrily at him. "Why do you think that's so funny?"

"Because when you first met her, she looked more like a Sam than a Samantha."

Cassidy didn't know how to respond to his comment, as it was a true statement. "Yes, she did, but her beauty still shown through her boyish appearance."

Drew patted Cassidy on the back. "You've made her very happy so far, but if you should do anything to make her miserable, you will have to deal with the two of us."

Drew's statement infuriated Cassidy. "She's my wife and I plan to do everything in my power to give her a good life, but sometimes terrible things do happen."

"Just make sure you aren't the cause of those terrible things," Drew said angrily, his eyes full of the promise of retaliation.

Corey stepped in between the two men. "Enough of this, we're family now. We'll be living in the same house until we can get the second house done, so we need to learn to get along." He turned to his brother. "I can't remember the last time I've seen our sister this happy, so back off Cassidy."

"I just don't want to see her get hurt."

"Then stop fighting with her husband."

"Fine," Drew said, then he stomped off towards the barn.

Corey looked over at Cassidy. "I'm sorry he's so . . ." he started, but he couldn't seem to find the right word to describe Drew's actions.

"Corey, don't worry about it. I'd rather see Samantha's brother acting the way he is, than not giving a damn about her. Someday the love bug will bite him, then he'll know what it's like to be in love, and then it will be our turn to torment him."

Corey laughed. "I'm glad you understand. Now, let's get started on the plans for the house."

The next morning, Samantha woke to the sound of some sort of commotion outside her window, concerned there was trouble, she jumped up out of bed and hurried to the window. When she peeked outside, she gasped at the sight of all the men in the yard. She turned back towards the bed to call to Cassidy, but found her husband was gone. She quickly dressed and rushed outside to see what the hullabaloo was about in the yard.

When Samantha saw Cassidy, she rushed to him. "What are all these men doing here?" she asked as she looked around the area in front of the barn.

"Instead of an old fashion barn-raising, we're going to raise our new house."

"Oh, Cassidy!" she exclaimed excitedly. "We'll be in our home in no time at all."

"The house won't be as big at the Stoltes' place."

"I know, but it doesn't matter." To her it didn't, she just wanted a house to make into a home with her new husband. "I'm just happy to be able to have a home of my own."

"You do realize your brothers will be living with us until we can start on their house."

"Yes, but I can handle them."

Cassidy laughed. "What are you going to do threaten them with sleeping in the barn if they aren't good?"

Samantha giggled. "No, I'll threaten not to cook for them."

"You're a mean woman," he said teasingly, taking her hand into his. He smiled at her as his mind turned to last night and their invigorating lovemaking.

She hoped he was teasing, because she didn't like the idea of her new husband thinking badly of her. "No, I'm not mean."

He pulled her into his arms, not caring who was watching them. "Did you or did you not tell me *no* last night when I asked to make love to you?" he asked softly, making sure only she heard what he asked.

She chuckled. "Cassidy, we had already made love three times," she whispered, then blushed. "Besides, I was tired and wanted to get some sleep."

"I guess tonight we'll have to go to bed early."

"That would be nice," she said, thinking of getting some extra shut-eye.

"That way we can make love four times before morning."

Samantha's blush deepened as she quickly looked around them, hoping no one had overheard their conversation. When she saw they were alone, she took her fist and hit him in the arm. "Cassidy, that wasn't a very gentleman like thing to say to your new wife."

He leaned over and kissed her cheek. "I'm sorry. I shouldn't have said what I did, but I can't help what you do to me."

They quickly broke apart when Calvin and Daisy came running out of the house screaming with excitement of seeing a house being built. Esther hollered after the children, telling them to stay out of the men's way.

"Go help the men start on our home. The sooner it's started, the sooner, we'll be moving in."

Cassidy gave her another kiss, then started for the men. She watched him until she felt someone touch her arm. She quickly looked over to see Esther beside her, and gave her friend a smile. "Did you know about this?"

Esther nodded. "A couple of our neighbor came over to meet us while you and I were unpacking in the house the other day. The men got to talking and when Gerard told them we were going to build three more houses on the property, they said they would be back with more help. When they returned, they began preparing the land so it would be ready for today. First, they will lay the floor, then they'll start building the walls."

"Who paid for all the lumber?" she asked, assuming Esther would say it had been her brothers.

Esther remained quiet, unsure if she should be the one to tell her who it was or not. "You should talk to your husband."

"Cassidy paid for all of it?" she asked, surprised he hadn't said anything to her about it. "He didn't even hint about any of this. When did he do all this?"

Esther took hold of Samantha's shoulder with her hands. "Go talk to your husband," she said, then turned her around and pushed her in the direction of the men.

"Cassidy," Samantha called.

He turned when he heard his name being called, seeing her hurt expression as she came towards him, he knew he should have told her about the surprise himself. He hurried towards her, and when he reached her, he grabbed her and kissed her. After what he hoped was a passionate enough kiss to take her mind off the men working behind them, he removed his lips from hers.

"Why did you kiss me like that?" she asked, touching her hand to her lips. If they weren't in the middle of the yard with a dozen or more people, she would assume he wanted to take her to bed.

He gave her a childish grin. "I want to explain before you could yell at me."

"Why would you think I was going to scream at you?"

"I thought you were mad because I didn't tell you about what I'd done."

"I'm a bit hurt you didn't say something to me earlier about paying for the lumber, but I not mad."

"I wanted it to be a surprise."

"That it was." She smiled at him, knowing they were going to have a good life together.

"Besides, with the honeymoon and all, it sort of slipped my mind."

"I know we really don't know much about each other, but I'm surprise you had enough money to pay for all this lumber."

"I have had some bad experiences with getting involved with women who only wanted me for my money, so I usually don't talk about the amount of money I have."

"I'm sorry. That must have hurt."

"Yes, it did, but I got over it."

She put her hand on his arm. "You don't think that about me, do you?"

He laughed, thinking back to the time he'd thought she was a boy. "No, with you I had my mind on other things," he said, insinuating sex had been on his mind. When he saw her cheeks turn pink, he smiled at her.

"Cassidy, I'm glad, as I would feel bad if you thought I'd married you for your money."

He pulled her into his arms. "I know why you married me."

"Do you?" she asked, her eyes looking deeply into his as she waited for his response.

"Yes, as it's the same reason I married you." He watched as her eyes filled with tears. "Please don't cry."

"I'm just so happy you're in my life."

"I'm glad you're in mine."

It had taken the men three days of hard work to build the house, but it would have taken longer if there hadn't so many people helping. Tonight, was their first night in their new house and now Samantha was waiting for Cassidy to join her in bed.

She could hear movement in the room next to theirs and grimaced. If she could hear Corey getting ready for bed, she knew he would be able to hear them when she and Cassidy made love. Did that mean she and Cassidy would have to wait until the other house was built before they could make love again? She frowned at the thought, as she wanted her husband to make love to her tonight. When she didn't hear anything from Corey's side of the wall, she assumed he was in bed. Waiting for Cassidy to come to bed, she started counting to one hundred, when she reached it, and her husband still hadn't arrived, she got out of bed to check where he could be.

After she put on her robe, she left their room. Noticing both of her brothers' doors was closed, she began searching the house, and when she didn't find him anywhere inside, she stepped outside into the night. Seeing a light in the Stoltes barn, she walked towards it.

"Cassidy, are you here?" Before she knew it, she was being swept up into a pair of strong arms. She gasped, but relaxed when she stared into her husband's eyes. "What are you doing?"

"I thought I would have my way with you in the barn."

She laughed thinking he was teasing her, but when he didn't chuckle at his comment, she knew he'd meant what he'd said. "You want to make love to me in here?"

"It doesn't have your two brothers within ear shot of us."

She nodded, but she was still unsure about being naked in the barn where anyone could walk in on them. "Isn't it a bit open?" she asked as she looked around them.

"The hayloft is pretty nice."

"Won't my brothers wonder where we are?"

"No."

"No?" she asked. "Why won't they?" When she saw his redden cheeks, she knew he'd told her brothers about what they were going to be doing in the barn. Her eyes widened. "You told my brothers we were going to be out here in the barn mating like some kind of animal," she whispered.

"Now Samantha, I didn't exact use those words. Remember, we were originally going to spend our honeymoon out here."

Tears filled her eyes. "Yes, it's just that I'm embarrassed."

"I'm sorry," he said as he set her down on her feet. "I've made us a bed in the hayloft." He took hold her hand when he reached her.

She climbed up the ladder first, with her husband following. When she reached the top, she could see by the soft lantern glow that Cassidy had indeed made them a nice bed. She turned towards her husband and quickly pulled her off her robe, then her nightgown.

Cassidy quickly undressed, then grabbed his wife and gently placed her on the pile of blankets. No words were spoken between them, as their lips were too busy to allow words to pass through.

Afterwards they returned to the house and went to bed. Once there, he kissed her, then put his mouth next to her ear. "Sam, I love you."

She smiled as tears ran down her cheeks. "And I love you."

The next morning, Samantha was expecting her brothers to make a comment regarding the barn incident, but it wasn't mentioned and she was relieved. She just hoped her brothers' home would be built quickly as she didn't look forward to be having sex in the barn when winter came.

CHAPTER TWENTY

The morning of Gwen's party, Corey, Drew, Samantha, and Cassidy arrived together. While Samantha and Cassidy went to join some of the other families, the two brothers went in search of their hosts, as they wanted to thank them for inviting them to the party.

Drew stopped suddenly when his eyes fell on a woman standing with Gwen and her husband. He quickly put his hand on his brother's arm to stop him, as his heart started thumping in his chest, his tongue had gone so dry he could hardly swallow, as she was the most the beautiful woman he'd ever seen in his life. "Corey, I was wrong, as I now believe in love at first sight," Drew muttered dreamingly.

While Drew was looking at Krista, Corey had been admiring Rachelle who was talking with Jillian and a man he'd assumed was her new husband. At his brother words, Corey head swung towards his brother, assuming Drew had been looking at the same woman he'd been.

He was prepared to fight his brother, if necessary, as he wanted a chance with the unknown woman with Jillian, but when he saw his brother wasn't even looking in the same direction, Corey quickly realized his mistake.

He smiled at the knowledge he wouldn't have to compete with his brother for the woman who'd capture his attention. "Yes, I think I believe in it too."

Drew looked over at him, wondering what he meant by his statement. "What are you talking about?"

"I'm talking about the woman standing with Jillian."

"Let's go our separate ways to meet the young woman of our choice and met back later to compare notes," Drew said.

Corey nodded, quickly heading off to the meet the woman before someone else walked off with her. But before he could reach her, a young woman stepped in front of him and he practically ran into her.

"Hello, my name is Kira Wallace. Welcome to our town."

"Thank you. I'm Corey Tyson." He didn't want to be rude, but he didn't want to take time talking to this woman, as he wanted to be with the other one. She was pretty, but he didn't feel any attraction to her.

"Would you like to go for a walk?" she asked coyly.

"I'm sorry, but I'm on my way over to visit with some friends. Maybe later," he said, giving her a warm smile. He wanted to tell her he wouldn't ever be interested in her, but he was too polite to say so.

"I'll just come with you," she said boldly.

Corey thought this was a bit nervy for a stranger. "I'm sorry, I rather you didn't as I have a private matter to discuss with my friends." He turned and hurried away before she thought about following him.

Rachelle's attention had been captured by the young man as soon as he and his family had arrived. She wondered who he was, as she hadn't ever seen him before. When he started walking towards them, her heart began beating rapidly in her chest and her hands started sweating. As she continued to watch him, she wondered if he was married, and if so, where his wife was.

She was disappointed when Kira stopped him, thinking that now he met her, she wouldn't have a chance of ever meeting him, as Kira had a way with getting a man's attention. As she watched him gave Kira the brush off, she forced herself not to think maybe she might have a chance with him after all.

Corey was relieved when he finally reached his goal. "Jillian, congratulations on your wedding. I came over to meet your new husband," he said, hoping she didn't know the real reason he was there. When Jillian smiled a knowing grin at him, he realized he hadn't fooled her, not one little bit.

She smiled sweetly. "This is my husband, Skyler Emery."

The two men shook hands. "It's nice to meet you. I'm glad to see you save Jillian from her father's plans."

"Me too."

"And this is Skyler's cousin Rachelle," she said, forcing herself not to smile as she introduced them.

Corey took hold of Rachelle's hand. "It's nice to meet you. Do you live around here?"

"Yes, I live with my parents." She cringed, as the words had simply jumped out of her mouth. "Where do you live?" she quickly asked, hoping to take the attention of her statement.

"I live on the Stolte ranch with my brother, Drew and our sister, Samantha and her husband Cassidy. Would you like to go for a walk? I could tell you about our trip here."

Rachelle smiled at him. "I would like that," she muttered, relieved to know he still lived with family too.

As the coupled walked off together, Jillian and Skyler smiled a knowing grin at each other, knowing the love bug had stuck again.

As Drew hurried towards their hosts to meet the woman with them before she could move away, he didn't notice the two women sizing him up. Just before he could reach Gwen and her husband, the two stepped in front of him.

"Hello. My name is Harriet Talcott, and this is my friend, Jayne Reid. We were wondering if you would like to join us at our table."

"Thank you for asking, but I've already made plans." He gave them a smile, then hurried on. When he reached Gwen and her husband, all he could do was stare at the woman standing next to Tucker, which cause her to blush.

"Hello Drew. Was there something you wanted?" Gwen asked the love-struck man.

Drew ignored Gwen, instead kept his eyes on Krista. "Hello, my name is Drew Tyson. My sister, brother, and I were on the wagon train with Gwen," he said as he put his hand out to her. When she took his hand, the sensation he felt made him think he'd died and gone to heaven.

"I'm Krista Owens. My brother, Tucker and I knew Gwen when she lived here as a child."

"How nice," he commented absentmindedly. "Would you like to get some punch?"

Krista gave him a nod. "I would like that."

The two moved away, leaving a smiling Gwen and Tucker behind. "Did you see how he disregarded those other two women who stopped him on his way to your sister?" she asked happily.

Tucker smiled. "Maybe Krista won't be a widow all that much longer."

"I hope you're right."

The rest of the day found the two Tyson brothers busy with Rachelle and Krista, causing the other three women to fume at the men's choices.

Not to be put off, the other three women conspired among themselves to get the two men's attention, but it didn't do them any good as four weeks later, Corey and Drew announced they were getting married to the woman they'd meet at Gwen and Tucker's party.

Since Drew would be living at Krista's ranch after they were married, he gave his share of the land to Samantha and Corey. Corey and Cassidy told Drew they wanted to pay him for his share, but he refused, saying he had everything a man could want. Samantha finally talked Drew into accepting a cash settlement, stating he could use it for when his children started coming along.

Samantha was happy knowing her brothers had found someone special, and would be living nearby. Rachelle and Krista decided to have a double wedding, thrilled by the fact they would soon be sisters.

The two brides decided to have a small wedding, inviting a few of their friends and the families that had been on the wagon train with the grooms. After the wedding, there was a large party to celebrate the occasion, with the rest of the town joining them for the celebration.

During the celebration, Jillian and Samantha told their friends that in seven months they both would be having a baby. Then there were more congratulations and good wishes, and bets made as to which one would deliver first. There was a lot of teasing among the friends, giving the new brides a hard time, telling them they would be next to be in the family way.

EPILOGUE

Tucker had left early that morning to go over to his sister's place to help Drew with repairs on some of his fencing, and didn't have any idea when he may return. Thinking the baby wasn't due for another week, Gwen told Tucker to go on, as she would be fine at home alone. But an hour later, when the first contraction hit her, Gwen knew she was in trouble.

Thinking of how Andrea had almost given birth by herself, Gwen began to cry; worried she would have to deliver the baby without help. She had two choices, she could stay here and wait for her husband to return, or she could saddle one of the horses, and ride to Krista's ranch for help. Since she hadn't any idea how much time she had before the baby came, she thought it was best to start for Krista's home before it was too late for her to ride a horse.

Gwen grabbed an apple from the kitchen table, then hurried to the barn. Going to the first stall, she held out her hand out with the apple on it, talking softly to the old mare that had been hers as a child. "Betsy, I need your help."

As the horse chomped on the apple, Gwen entered the stall. Once there, she turned and stared at the saddle, unsure if she could throw it over the back of the horse in her condition. Knowing she couldn't risk riding the horse bareback, she waited until the next contraction had passed, and once it had, she grabbed the saddle, and flung it over the back of the horse.

She jumped when Betsy nipped at her arm, wanting another apple. "You are going to have to wait until later."

Then in between contractions, she was able to cinch the strap under the horse's belly and mount her. The contractions were starting to come faster and more intense now, and she wasn't sure if she would be able to reach help before the baby made its appearance. She said a quick prayer, asking God to let her get to Krista's ranch before the baby came.

Shortly after saying her prayer, the contractions seemed to stop, but she wasn't about to question why. She started the horse down the road at a steady pace, and when she saw Krista's home, she let out a shaky breath, relieved to know her ride was almost over.

She stopped in front of the house, and then by holding tight on the saddle horn, she carefully lowered herself from Betsy's back. Once she had her feet on the ground, she leaned her head against the horse's neck, giving her a good hug.

"I'll make sure you get an apple as soon as I can, but right now, I'm going to find Krista and have this baby." She tied the reins to the hitching post, then moved to the front door and opened it. "Krista, are you here?"

Krista came running out from the back of the house. "Gwen, what on earth are you doing here?"

"The baby's coming."

Krista rushed to Gwen and put her arm around her. "Let's get you to bed."

"Yes, please."

"How did you get here?"

"I rode a horse."

She looked shocked. "While in labor?"

Gwen laughed. "I didn't have much of a choice. Luckily, the contraction stopped and I was able to get here without a lot of pain. I promised Betsy an apple if she got me here in time."

"I'll give her two. Now hush and save your strength for birthing your child."

Gwen looked at her sister-in-law closely, and noticing a special glow about her, she gave her a secret smile. "You're pregnant, aren't you?"

"Yes, but don't say anything to anyone, as I haven't had a chance to tell Drew about the baby yet."

"What are you waiting for?"

"If he knows I'm pregnant, he'll want me to stop working around the ranch and that's something I don't want happening."

Gwen shook her head. "I thought you had Drew wrapped around your little finger."

Krista laughed. "I didn't think anyone knew that."

"I'm sure if you explain how important working on the ranch is to you, he'll understand."

"You never know just how men are going to react to the news of being a father. Now, let go have a little one."

Tucker and Drew had just stepped into the house when they heard a baby cry. They gave each other a puzzled look, then hurried to where the sound had come from.

When they stepped into Drew's bedroom and Tucker saw his wife in the bed, he rushed to her side, taking hold of her hand. "Are you all, right?"

She gave him a reassuring smile. "I'm fine now.

"Gwen, how did you get here?"

"I rode Betsy here." She turned to Krista. "Don't forget to give her two apples."

Krista patted her arm. "I gave her the apples when I moved her into the barn."

"Oh, I don't remember you leaving me."

Krista smiled at her. "You were resting after Grayden was born."

Tucker gasped. "You named your son after my father?"

Gwen had been assured by Krista it would be all right, but by her husband's expression, she wasn't too sure now at her choice of name for her son.

"If you rather he had a different name, I can change it."

"No, I'm touched you want to give your son my father's name."

"I thought the name might help you feel that he's your son too."

"Gwen, it doesn't matter what his name is, as I've thought of him as mine since the day we were married."

She smiled at him. "I'm glad." She was confused when her husband gave her a funny look. "What is it?"

"I just wonder if the baby had been a girl, would you have named her after the horse you rode over here."

Drew and Krista sniggered at his comment.

"Betsy is a wonderful name and I'm sure the horse would have been honored to have my daughter named after her."

"Yes, I'm sure you're right." He smiled at the other two. "Just don't tell the horse that, otherwise she'd be disappointed that you had a boy."

Gwen rolled her eyes at his comment. "Men!"

"I guess you're going to be staying here for a few days."

"If I can ride over here in labor, I can ride home with a baby in my arms," she stated determinedly.

Tucker chuckled. "I don't think that will be necessary. You rest for a couple of days, then I'll take you home in the wagon."

Three days later, Gwen went home sitting next to her husband in their wagon, with their son in her arms. She was surprised when they arrived at the ranch to find the yard filled with several other wagons.

As she looked around at all the faces, she saw all her friends from the wagon train and their spouses there. Tables were set up and soon everyone was eating food the women had brought with them. After everyone was done eating, Gwen stood and faced her friends.

"Thank you all for being here. I also want to thank Jillian, Andrea, and Samantha who befriended me months ago, as their friendship was what got me through those days on the trail. I also want to thank Tucker for rescuing me after my husband's death."

Everyone knew how he was more or less responsible for Felix's death, but she didn't want to dwell on that, so she went on. "His sister, Krista, became my sister, and when she married her husband, he too became my family. I want to thank Krista for delivering our son." She had to stop as her tears had caused her throat to close up.

"Don't forget to thank Betsy," her husband called out.

Everyone laughed, as they all knew who Betsy was and why she should be included.

"Yes, I thank Betsy too. As if it wasn't for her, I would have given birth at home by myself. Again, I thank you all for being my family."

Jillian, Andrea, and Samantha stood and joined Gwen, their arms circling around the person next to them. At the beginning to their trip westward, their lives seemed gloomy and bleak. Andrea and Gwen were in bad marriages, Jillian was expected to marry a man she didn't know, and probably never would love, while Samantha had just lost her parents.

The husbands stood and joined their wives, Blake handed a fussy Grace over to her mother, and Tucker laid his sleeping son in his mother's arms, while Cassidy and Skyler embraced their wives.

Now the four women were all happily married to wonderful men and their lives were as rewarding as any woman could hope for, as they loved their husbands and they loved them.

Their journey westward had been over for several months, but now they had a different type of journey ahead of them, one that included their husbands and children.

BOOKS WRITTEN
by Cheri LePage

Sara's Story

Will You Marry Me?

The Long Way Home

Wildfire

My New Beginnings

Are You My Sister?

Three Prescott Brides

Her Lost Love

I'm Not Amanda

Three Lost & Found Babies

Kiera's Catch 22

Paige's Predicament

Sea Hawk

Westward Wagons

Marissa's Second Chance

DNA Doesn't Lie

The Wee Care Abduction

A Road to Consequences

Secrets

www.ingramcontent.com/pod-product-compliance
Lightning Source LLC
LaVergne TN
LVHW010201070526
838199LV00062B/4450